The
Frindle
Files

Favorites by Andrew Clements

About Average

Extra Credit

The Friendship War

Frindle

The Jacket

The Landry News

The Last Holiday Concert

The Losers Club

Lost and Found

Lunch Money

The Map Trap

No Talking

The Report Card

The School Story

Troublemaker

A Week in the Woods

and many others!

The Frindle Files

Andrew Clements

DECORATIVE ART BY **B**rian **S**elznick

RANDOM HOUSE 🏠 NEW YORK

The publisher wishes to thank Stephanie Peters for her thoughtful editorial work to help prepare this manuscript for publication.

Visit us on the Web! rhcbooks.com

Educators and librarians, for a variety of teaching tools,
visit us at RHTeachersLibrarians.com

Library of Congress Cataloging-in-Publication Data is available upon request.
ISBN 978-0-399-55763-7 (trade)—ISBN 978-0-399-55764-4 (lib. bdg.)—
ISBN 978-0-399-55765-1 (ebook)

Jacket art painted in acrylics on watercolor paper.
Interior decorations drawn entirely with a *frindle*.
The text of this book is set in 12-point Horley Old Style MT Pro.

Editor: Michelle H. Nagler
Designer: Jade Rector
Copy Editor: Barbara Bakowski
Managing Editor: Rebecca Vitkus
Production Manager: Tim Terhune

Printed in the United States of America
10 9 8 7 6 5 4 3 2 1
First Edition

Thank you, Andrew!

From Becky, Charles,
George, Nate, and John

17. Omit needless words.

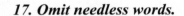

Vigorous writing is concise. A sentence should contain no unnecessary words, a paragraph no unnecessary sentences, for the same reason that a drawing should have no unnecessary lines and a machine no unnecessary parts. This requires not that the writer make all sentences short, or avoid all detail and treat subjects only in outline, but that every word tell.

—from *The Elements of Style,* 4th ed.,
by William Strunk Jr. and E. B. White

```
Simple is better than complex.
Complex is better than complicated.
Flat is better than nested.
Sparse is better than dense.
Readability counts.

-from "The Zen of Python" by Tim Peters
```

Chapter 1

Results

The only thing Josh Willett liked about homework was how quickly he could access his assignments. All he had to do was turn on his laptop, then click the SIXTH-GRADE HOMEWORK portal he'd bookmarked on his browser at the start of the school year.

This system let Josh zoom through his homework so he could get back to the things he cared about most—like a new coding problem, or a new digital animation project, or a new action sequence for the online game he wanted to build. Because Josh always had something new to work on, a plan he was hatching. And usually, it involved his computer.

On this Monday evening in mid-September, without taking his fingers off the keyboard or his eyes off the screen,

Josh sat at the kitchen table and crushed his homework for math, science, and social studies in less than twenty minutes—including the time it took to post each finished assignment.

Then he clicked the link for his ELA class.

The image of a handwritten note popped open on his screen:

Homework due Tuesday
Describe something you think is beautiful.
Make your description at least one hundred words long. Avoid clichés, and remember this advice from page 70 of *The Elements of Style:* "Write in a way that comes naturally." Copy your final draft onto lined paper in blue or black ink, and turn in the assignment Tuesday at the beginning of class. As always, neatness counts.
Mr. N

The assignment itself, plus the way it had been written by hand, plus the whole "neatness counts" thing? All of it made Josh scowl and grit his teeth. A chore like this should only take about ten minutes: type it, format it, spellcheck it, post it, and *whoosh!* Done.

But having to write out every language arts assignment in ink on *paper*? It was annoying, slow, and totally pointless—not to mention bad for the environment. Didn't Mr. N understand *anything*?

It wasn't that Mr. N was mean or unfair. He just seemed so backward. And also dull—except for the way he dressed.

He owned at least ten Hawaiian shirts, and he wore one each day, along with surfer shorts, hiking socks, and sandals. He would wear cargo pants, but only if the outdoor temperature got below sixty-five degrees. His dark red hair never looked completely tamed, especially when he rode his bike to school. Some days it seemed like he was trying to grow a mustache. Or a beard. Or both. Plenty of people in Southern California wore casual clothes, but at Clara Vista Middle School? Mr. N could win a prize for Least-Dressed-Up Teacher every single day.

The most backward thing about Mr. N? He was the only teacher in the whole school who didn't let kids use laptops in class. He claimed there was no rule saying he had to allow them. Josh had checked the school handbook after getting the first assignment, just to make sure.

Josh wasn't sure if Mr. N even owned a computer. There was a rumor that once he'd had a big argument with Mr. Ortega about posting his homework assignments on the school website. Mr. N had told the principal that writing assignments on the board in his classroom was enough—and he didn't mean one of the SMART Boards that every other teacher used. No, Mr. N had an actual chalkboard that he could move around the room on wheels. The whiteboard was there, but Mr. N kept it hidden behind a huge poster about the parts of speech.

And that miserable little grammar book, *The Elements of Style?* Most of it was over a hundred years old.

Almost every day Mr. N made the entire class open to a certain page, and then some poor kid would have to stand up and read something out loud. If you forgot to bring your copy to class, you'd get a red mark in the grade book—and three marks made your whole grade drop five points.

Antique books, ancient chalkboards, handwriting on paper—Mr. N's class felt like being stuck inside a broken time machine. . . . More like a time-*wasting* machine. It was so frustrating to Josh, who just wanted Mr. N to appreciate the world his students were *actually* living in.

But grumbling was also a waste of time, so Josh opened a new document on his laptop. He had to write out the final copy by hand, but he always *typed* his first draft—like a normal human being living in the twenty-first century.

Something beautiful . . .

Josh stared at the empty document on his screen, watching the cursor as it blinked and blinked. He had no ideas, not even a bad one.

But as he looked at that blinking cursor, he decided it must be appearing once each second—a half second on, a half second off. He opened the stopwatch app on his iPhone and ran a quick test.

Yup, one blink per second.

And Josh understood why.

The cursor blinked once each second because somewhere inside his laptop there was a line or two of computer code. A programmer had written that code, which told the computer what to do. And the computer obeyed—it had no choice. Because good code is like a set of unbreakable rules. And if the programmer gets everything right, that code keeps working, and working *perfectly,* practically forever, and . . .

And that's *what I'm going to write about!*

A few hours earlier during his after-school coding club, Josh had finished writing a perfect Python loop statement— a sequence of instructions that repeated itself until a specific goal was met. And that loop was *beautiful!* A flurry of words rushed into his mind, and Josh's fingers zipped around the keyboard. Six or seven minutes later, the counter at the bottom of his document showed he had typed 136 words, just like that.

After some quick proofreading, he began writing his final copy on a sheet of lined paper. Neatly. Josh knew he had scrunchy handwriting. But his spelling was perfect, and his sentences made sense. The page looked clean and organized, and word after word flowed onto the paper in bright blue ink.

With only four sentences left to copy, disaster struck. The pen skipped, and the dry point almost tore his paper— it was out of ink.

Josh shook the pen and tried it again. Nothing.

He banged it on the edge of the kitchen table, but that didn't help either, so he dug around in his backpack and found two other pens.

He tested one on a scrap of paper. Black ink.

He tried the second. More black ink—and he needed blue ink to match what he'd started with for Mr. N, the neatness nut.

I guess I could start over and use black ink . . . ?

Josh shouted, "Hey, *Mom?*"

"I'm right here, and quiet down—Dad's putting Sophie to bed."

Josh hurried through the doorway into the family room.

"I need a pen with blue ink so I can finish Mr. N's homework."

"Check the middle drawer of my desk."

Josh opened the drawer, and the first pen he tried? Blue ink.

"Got one—thanks!"

Back at the kitchen table, Josh was about to start writing again. Then he noticed something printed on the side of the pen—one word, in bold black letters:

It was a word he'd never seen before, which made him curious. And Josh did what any other plugged-in kid would do: He searched the word on his browser—*f-r-i-n-d-l-e*. And then he hit return.

Whoa, 270,000 results?!

After clicking a few links, Josh opened up the images that were part of the search results—a *lot* of images. The very first picture showed some kid on a TV talk show, smiling at the camera and holding up a pen. And in another image halfway down his screen, Josh saw a close-up of a pen that was *exactly* like his mom's!

He dashed back to the family room.

"Hey, Mom, where did you get this pen?"

She looked, and then smiled. "I've had that since sixth grade. Everyone at my school started calling pens frindles, and when those showed up in stores, I bought a couple—so did all my friends. It was kind of a big thing for a while."

"Is it okay if I use this one to finish my homework?"

"Sure, but then put it back, please. That might be a collector's item someday."

Josh hurried back to the table to finish his homework, shaking the old pen as he went. Three minutes later he was done with his final draft, and even though the ink from his mom's pen wasn't a perfect match, it was definitely blue.

He returned the pen to her desk, then went back to his computer. The picture results were still on his screen, and Josh clicked the photo of that kid holding up his pen on a talk show. The enlarged image gave him a good look at the boy—red hair, glasses, freckles, and a wide smile.

Josh read the words below the picture: **Nicholas Allen, age 11, inventor of the word** *frindle.*

"Cool," he whispered, impressed that a kid his age was an inventor.

He looked at the boy's face, and then leaned in closer to the screen, still looking.

Josh whispered, "No *way!*"

He clicked back to his homework assignment page, then back to the school's home page. He kept clicking links until there was a second photo open on his screen, and he put the two pictures side by side—the boy on the left, and the new photo on the right.

Then Josh almost stopped breathing. The kid on the left was eleven, and the man on the right was at least thirty, but Josh was sure he was looking at two photos of the same person.

And that man on the right? It was his language arts teacher, Mr. N—also known as Mr. Allen Nicholas.

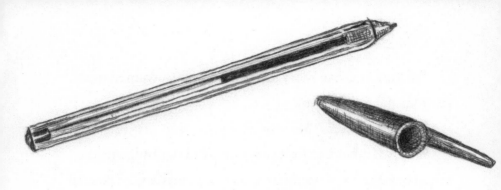

Chapter 2

Binary Question

Josh loved writing programs for computers, because computers demanded perfection. The answer to the question "Does this program work?" had to be either YES or NO. It was never MAYBE.

He also loved how computers made billions of exact calculations every second by using binary code. Binary code was so simple—nothing but ones and zeroes. Those ones and zeroes worked like tiny switches inside a computer, and those switches were either ON or OFF—just like YES or NO. Never MAYBE.

So when Josh had a problem to solve, he usually tried to turn it into a binary question—a simple question with only two possible answers, like TRUE or FALSE, YES or NO.

And on Tuesday morning at school, Josh wanted to answer *this* binary question:

Mr. N and Nick Allen: Are they IDENTICAL or DIFFERENT?

The night before, Josh had started to doubt his discovery about Mr. N—maybe it was all a coincidence. And to cure this uncertainty, Josh had done more research and kept careful records of what he found.

After taking another long look at those two pictures—the kid holding up his frindle, and Mr. N's photo from the school website—Josh had dragged a copy of each onto his desktop, along with one of the frindle pen images. He discovered an old article about Nick Allen and *frindle* in the *Westfield Gazette,* the newspaper in the kid's hometown; then an article about Nick's fifth-grade English teacher, Mrs. Granger; and a third article about Bud Lawrence, the man who had started a company to sell those frindle pens all over the country. With so many links to explore, after only half an hour Josh had copied over fifty different photos, articles, and documents onto his desktop.

Josh actually had two desktops: the digital desktop on his computer screen, and the physical desktop on a desk in his bedroom—and his physical desktop was a wreck. Along with all the papers, notepads, pens, and pencils, there were also coding books and manuals, used worksheets, a copy of

Josh Willett

this year's school photo, his dad's old calculator, a plastic flowchart template, at least a dozen scattered yellow sticky notes, plus two broken hard drives, a tangle of cables and power cords, and a camera he hadn't used since he'd gotten half an iPhone for his twelfth birthday gift— his mom and dad had paid for half, and he had paid for the other half with money he'd been saving since the beginning of fourth grade.

The desktop in his room had been cluttered for years, but the desktop on his computer? Josh cleaned it up at least once a day. His laptop was crammed with thousands of photos and assignments and apps and documents and programs and projects, but all of them were tucked away inside labeled folders. Whenever his digital desktop got messy or crowded, it was never a problem because the fix was only a few clicks away.

And on Monday night, all of Josh's research—a jumble

of JPEGs and DOCs and PDFs—neatly vanished from his home screen into a new folder. Josh smiled as he typed a name for this folder: THE FRINDLE FILES. It sounded like a Netflix series about a secret investigation, or maybe a sci-fi thriller about alien robots.

There were fifty-three items in this folder, and all but a handful were about that boy, Nick Allen. Josh had information about how the word *frindle* had been invented, how it had spread across the country, how teachers from Maine to Hawaii had tried to stop kids from using the word, and how millions of people had bought frindle pens and T-shirts and caps.

It had been simple to track Nick Allen online. He started out in Westfield, New Hampshire, and eventually went to college at the University of Massachusetts. Josh had even found a front-page article about Nick from the student newspaper: **UMass Freshman Created Frindle.** But after college? Nothing. It was as if Nick Allen had gone off to live alone in the woods—or been abducted by alien robots.

Josh had found only three items about Mr. N that seemed worth keeping: that school website photo; an article from four years ago in the *Clara Vista Condor* about new teachers in town; and another brief news story showing him and his wife and their newborn daughter. All the other information he'd found was more recent stuff about Mr. N at the middle school.

Josh had also worked out a rough timeline: Nicholas Allen had finished college in 2009, then disappeared, and Mr. Allen Nicholas had popped up in Clara Vista, California—*eight years later!* It was quite a mystery—and the name for his data folder seemed like a perfect fit.

But Josh had also realized that unless he could *prove* that Nick Allen and Mr. N were IDENTICAL, all this digital information meant nothing. And by bedtime on Monday, he had come up with a plan to continue his research the next morning at school—in real life.

■ ▢ ▧ ◼   ◼ ▢ ▢ ◼

After first-period gym on Tuesday, Josh hurried and arrived early for language arts. He had that picture on his phone of Nick Allen holding up his frindle on TV, and he wanted to compare it to the actual Mr. N.

When he got to his seat in room 113, he sneaked a peek at his phone. Then Josh studied Mr. N, sitting there at his desk making notes in his *Elements of Style* paperback.

Mr. N had the same color hair and eyes as the boy, same shape nose and mouth, and they both wore round-rimmed glasses. And, of course, their names were remarkably similar. . . . Actually, *too* similar. If a person named Nicholas Allen had wanted to change his name, why would he just swap the parts around? That seemed almost stupid, and Josh knew Mr. N was intelligent.

In spite of their similar appearances and names, Josh the Programmer needed perfect binary clarity: Are they IDENTICAL or DIFFERENT? So he waited for the right moment to put a plan in motion.

At precisely 8:23, Josh walked to the bookcase in the front corner of the room. Mr. N was always going on about how reading good books makes you a better writer, and his shelves were overflowing. Josh pulled out a copy of *Tuck Everlasting* and stood there pretending to read the back cover. He felt like a detective on a stakeout.

Exactly one minute later, Mr. N got up and went out to stand in the hallway next to his door, something he did right before each class.

Josh waited another thirty-nine seconds, then put the book back and walked toward his seat—but as he passed Mr. N's desk, he pulled something from his pocket and slipped it underneath Mr. N's *Elements of Style*.

Josh got to his chair just as the bell rang. He took out his homework assignment, the one written on lined paper in two different shades of blue ink. He also found his copy of *The Elements of Style* in case he needed to prove he had brought it to class. He dug around in his backpack for a fresh pencil and a piece of paper so he'd be all set to take notes.

And then Josh wished he had a hundred other little tasks so he could keep busy for the next fifty-three minutes. That way, he might look like a regular kid during a regular ELA class—a kid who wasn't nervous, or worried, or half out of his skull with excitement.

Because Josh had just set a trap.

Using a fine-tipped Sharpie, he had written the word *Frindle* in bold black letters along the barrel of a plain white plastic pen. And now that word on that pen was right there on that desk, waiting for Mr. N to discover it. And when he did, Josh would be watching.

Nick Allen and Mr. N were either IDENTICAL or DIFFERENT—either the same person or not—and the answer to this binary question was coming.

Soon.

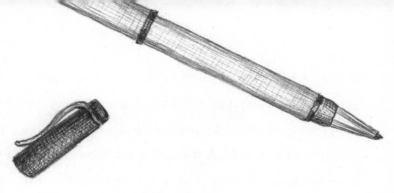

Chapter 3

Answer

Josh's trap wasn't working. Mr. N hadn't been anywhere near his desk all period, and ELA was nearly over.

They had been learning about adverbs, which was only half the problem. The other half was Mr. N himself. He was trying to be funny today, and once he got started down that road, he was almost impossible to stop.

Mr. N had been wandering around the room, but now he stood next to his green chalkboard near the windows, writing random words on it as he talked.

"Adverbs are useful, but they can also be dangerous. *How* dangerous? Seriously dangerous. Endlessly dangerous. Terrifyingly dangerous. And *when* does this adverb danger happen? It happens often. It happened yesterday.

In fact, it's happening right now. And *where* does this danger happen? It happens here, and there, and everywhere. It happens inside, outside, upstairs. . . ."

Josh had to do something. Mr. N was sure to find that homemade frindle pen today, but unless Josh was in the room to actually *see* him react to it, the trap was pointless—and he wouldn't get an answer to his question.

There must be a way to—

Faster than words, he had an idea.

Mr. N didn't like interruptions, but Josh raised his hand anyway, and waited. And waited.

Mr. N finally nodded at him, and Josh said, "Is there anything in *The Elements of Style* about adverbs?"

Mr. N looked so happy about this question that Josh was afraid he might do a little dance. Because if Mr. N got wound up enough, he would sometimes slide into a dance move. The school year was less than a month old, and he had already done this twice—and totally embarrassed everyone. Except himself.

"*Great* question, Josh, and the answer is *yes*! In the last chapter of the book, E. B. White has all kinds of good advice about using adverbs. Actually, my favorite bit might be in Reminder Four, and I believe there's also something in Reminder Eleven."

Then Mr. N hurried over and reached for the little book on his desk—and as he picked it up, Josh's fake frindle dropped to the floor.

The pen rolled a few feet toward the kids in the front row, but if Mr. N saw it, he ignored it. He flipped through his book and began reading the parts about adverbs.

Josh didn't hear a word. He was trying not to look at the floor, and at the same time he was mentally yelling, *Pick up that pen! Pick it up* now!

The silent shouting didn't work.

When he finished reading, Mr. N glanced at the clock. "Well, I have managed to grind up fifty-two minutes into grammatically correct sausage. If I don't have your home-work paper yet, please put it here on my desk before you leave."

Vanessa Ames got out her assignment and stood up to turn it in. Then, as Josh watched, she reached down, picked up the runaway pen, and handed it to Mr. N.

"This fell off your desk."

Mr. N smiled and said, "Thanks."

Josh saw Mr. N look at the pen, saw his eyes focus on that single word. The expression on Mr. N's face flashed from recognition, to confusion, and then to something that looked almost like fear—a reaction that surprised Josh.

And then just that quickly, it was as if nothing had happened. The look of fear vanished almost instantly, and Mr. N tucked the pen into the pocket of his shorts.

But something had happened, and Josh thought he saw a sudden sharpness in Mr. N's eyes as he looked around the classroom.

Josh turned away, trying not to grin. He kept his face blank as he put all his thought and energy into the small job of clearing his desk and loading his backpack. And as he dropped his homework assignment onto Mr. N's desk, Josh risked a glance at his teacher.

That one look turned Josh from triumphant to troubled. Because he realized that Mr. N knew something. In this second-period class of twenty-three students, *one kid* had slipped that pen onto his desk. *One kid* knew about his connection with *frindle*.

And now Mr. N was on the hunt.

The bell rang, and Josh tried to seem loose and natural as he left the room and headed for math. He relaxed for real once he had turned the corner of the hallway. And he grinned as in his mind he shouted the answer to his binary question: *Are Nick Allen and Mr. N the same person?*

YES!

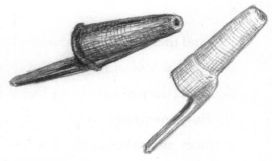

Chapter 4

The Ghost of Frindle

Vanessa Ames caught up with Josh in the hall after class.

"So, am I the only one who saw Mr. N freak out back there?"

Josh nearly tripped over his feet.

"What are you talking about?"

"About Mr. N's face. When I handed him that pen, he got spooked. I mean, he didn't cross his eyes or start barking, but for half a second it was like he'd seen a ghost or something, a total nanopanic. Did you see it too?"

Josh realized he was not surprised that Vanessa had noticed Mr. N's face. She didn't miss much. Her family had moved to Clara Vista in the middle of fourth grade, and on her very first day she had scanned every kid in the cafeteria with her hi-def radar, and then picked Josh as the one person who absolutely would not mind if she just walked over, sat down, and started talking—which was what she'd done. And she had been right.

Josh and Vanessa usually laughed about the same stuff, they liked a lot of the same books and games, and they were both into skateboarding and trail biking. They had also tried skimboarding at Venice Beach one day last summer— and failed miserably. And then laughed about it.

One thing they did *not* have in common? Vanessa was good with computers, but she didn't love everything about them the way Josh did. Even though he had never been able to get her hooked on coding, she had become one of his best friends anyway.

Still, Josh wasn't sure he should tell her this secret.

But she had just asked him a question, so he had to say something.

"Yeah," Josh said, "I saw the same freeze-up."

She said, "Okay, so here's what I think. I saw something

Vanessa Ames

written on that pen I handed him, a word—*tremble* or something? I don't know why, but maybe he had a reaction to it. Weird, huh?"

Now Josh was stuck.

If he told Vanessa about the word on the pen, that was the key, and it might lead her into the whole secret. But if he didn't tell her now, and she learned about it later? Then she'd know he had held back.

And holding back a secret like this from Vanessa? Not cool.

He stopped her at the door of his math classroom before she could head to her social studies class. He looked both ways, then kept his voice low. "I can't explain everything now, but if you get a second, google the word *frindle*—spelled *f-r-i-n-d-l-e*. Then go to the images, and check out the first picture in the results. And we have to keep *all* of this totally between us, okay?"

Vanessa's eyes lit up. "A mystery *and* a secret—I love it! My lips are sealed. See you at lunch!"

Josh went to his seat, but as he took out his laptop and got ready for class, a pesky binary question popped into his mind:

Telling Vanessa about frindle: *Was that* BAD *or* GOOD?

Josh did not like the answer he came up with.

Chapter 5

Decision Tree

When Vanessa walked into the cafeteria and began to look around for him, Josh could tell she had figured out that Nick Allen and Mr. N were the same person. And when their eyes met, she made a face at him—a huge silent scream.

Josh had decided he was glad about telling Vanessa. Knowing this on his own had felt like a heavy weight, but now it had turned into something fun, more like an adventure.

And then Vanessa sat down and started talking.

"*Unbelievable!* Seeing the picture of that kid, and then putting it all together? If you had tried to explain this, I would have laughed it off! And that pen I handed him, that was from *you*, right?"

Josh said, "Yeah, I—" but Vanessa didn't stop.

"So, here's what we do: We go to Mr. N's room right after school and lay it all out there—that we know every-thing about him and *frindle*, that we think it's totally *amazing*, and that we want to tell *everybody*. I mean, it's completely *wild*, don't you think? How he made up a new word like that, and went on TV and stuff? He's a *celeb-rity*, and nobody else even knows it! If *I'd* done some-thing that fantastic, I'd get a special license plate—maybe FRINDLE BOSS or FRINDLE ON! Plus, what's the deal with his name? Is he Nicholas Allen or is he Allen Nicholas? But we can just ask him! I say we crash into his room and hit him with the whole enchilada. What could go wrong?"

Miguel dropped into the seat next to Vanessa. "Wrong with what?"

"What's wrong? Is something wrong?" That was Hunter, sitting down beside Josh. And now their regular lunch crew was complete.

Josh thought fast. "Just talking about Mr. N's dance moves."

"And his flowered shirts!" Vanessa added, shooting Josh a conspiratorial look.

"Oh." Hunter rolled his eyes. "Yeah, those are wrong, all right! But even worse? Handwriting his assignments! That guy ruins my life every single night."

That comment started an avalanche of gripes, first about Mr. N's antitech ways, and then about Mrs. Coleman, and how she tried to turn every science class into a super-dramatic TED Talk.

Josh listened, but he was mostly thinking about Vanessa's idea: the two of them, face to face with Mr. N, right after school, talking about *frindle.* Today.

Mr. N had not looked happy when he saw the word on that pen, and popping in to make him talk about it seemed like asking for trouble.

Josh knew Vanessa wanted to get right up into Mr. N's nostrils about this. She always wanted to charge ahead, to go all in . . . like with that skimboarding disaster last summer? Completely her idea. "No, we really *have* to try it—I'll get my mom to take us to the beach today! What could go wrong?"

A face-plant into the sand, that's *what—which left me wearing a plastic nose flap for three weeks. Not cool.*

When Vanessa and Josh had a few minutes by themselves on the playground after lunch, he said, "I get what you're saying about us talking to Mr. N, but you saw him this morning. No way he wants to talk about this, right? Can we text tonight, see if we come up with anything else?"

"Yeah, sure," Vanessa said. "That's fine."

Josh knew she was disappointed, but then she smiled and said, "So, how about you build a decision tree, test all the branching options, and maybe by Halloween you can work up an algorithm that'll tell us exactly what our next move should be!"

"Ha ha—very funny."

It *was* funny, and Josh couldn't help smiling. Vanessa teased him about coding almost every day.

But Josh also knew she was close to the truth. He hated jumping into anything without thinking it through. Even when he did have a plan, things sometimes went wrong. Like this morning. He had gotten a reaction from Mr. N that confirmed his suspicions. But he hadn't counted on Mr. N looking upset, or searching the room for the person who left the frindle on his desk.

He had no clue what their next move should be, or even if there should be a move at all. Because doing nothing was always a possible move . . . more of a nonmove, really—like a zero in binary code, instead of a one.

Josh kept wondering and worrying the rest of the afternoon. But all of that turned out to be unnecessary.

The next move had already been made.

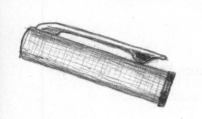

Chapter 6

X, Y, and Z

When Josh was about halfway home on the bus after school, he got a text from Vanessa.

Did you check out Mr. N's homework?

He answered right back:

No.

Then Vanessa wrote,

Text me when you do—if you are not on the floor.

It took Josh about fifteen seconds to find the school's website on his phone and open the assignment.

Homework due Wednesday
Imagine that Person X has discovered a secret about Person Y—nothing bad, but something that all of X's friends would find interesting. However, X also learns that Y would rather *not* have this secret made public.

In one or two paragraphs totaling no more than 150 words, explain what you think Person X might do with this secret, and why. Bring your final draft to class tomorrow, written in blue or black ink on lined paper. As usual, neatness counts. And don't forget about Reminder 16 from Chapter V of *The Elements of Style:* "Be clear."
Mr. N

Josh didn't fall out of his seat on the bus, but he was having trouble catching his breath. Was Mr. N—also known as Person Y—using the assignment to figure out who had planted the frindle? Or was he warning Person X to back off, to not reveal his secret? Or both? He replied to Vanessa's text to show he'd found it. He thought about using the scream face but picked the surprised emoji instead.

Right away, Vanessa sent a new text:

> Person X!!! You were right. Person Y would NOT have wanted to talk to us today. And Y would definitely be upset that you told someone. Which means we have another big secret—me!

Then another text:

> Hey—can my code name be Z??

Josh's mind was whirling. He couldn't think what to write back, so he sent emojis again—first a thumbs-up, and then, this time, he went ahead and used the scream.

When he got home twenty minutes later, Josh didn't get a snack, didn't open his favorite Python podcast, didn't watch YouTube, didn't do any of his usual after-school routines.

Instead, he sat down at the kitchen table, opened his laptop, and tried something completely new: He pulled up his ELA homework *first*—and reread the assignment. *Explain what you think Person X might do with this secret, and why.*

Josh stared at the screen for a long time, thinking. Then he smiled. And he began to type.

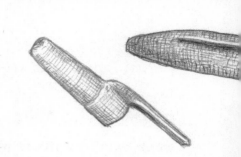

Chapter 7

On the Hunt

Wednesday was one of those days when Mr. N looked like he hadn't shaved. Or showered. And his hiking socks didn't match. He started class by walking around the room to collect the homework assignments from each kid, something he'd never done before.

Then he stood beside his desk and said, "Some of you might be wondering about last night's homework. Would anyone like to guess why I gave this assignment?"

Josh glanced around the room. No volunteers. He swallowed hard and tried to look like he wasn't interested. Or scared. Because Mr. N knew that one student in this class had understood the reason for this assignment *perfectly,* and now he was trying to flush that kid out into the open.

Mr. N said, "So far this year, most of your daily writing assignments have been about accurate description—also about learning to write with purpose, clarity, a suitable design, and so on."

"And about handwriting neatly in blue or black ink," Josh heard Hunter mutter.

"But for today," Mr. N continued, "I asked you to imagine a conflict between two people and then to explain what you think one of them might do—in this case, what Person X might do with Person Y's secret. And now we're going to do something else that's different."

Mr. N sat down with the homework papers, pulled one from the stack, and laid it on his desk.

"I'm going to read a few of your assignments aloud, but I'm not going to identify the writers. Please listen to the first one, and then we'll have a discussion."

Mr. N moved his glasses near the end of his nose and began to read.

Person X will probably tell a bunch of friends anyway. And if Person Y isn't very nice, maybe Person X will even put the secret out on social.

Mr. N looked up from the paper. "That's all this student wrote—which is fine, because I didn't assign a minimum number of words, only a maximum. Any thoughts about this brief statement?"

A lot of hands went up, and Mr. N pointed at Charlotte.

"Secrets *are* kind of fun to share, so X might reveal it. But I don't like the part about telling everyone on social media because Person Y maybe isn't very nice. That's mean."

Mr. N said, "Trevor, what do you think?"

"Yeah, telling everyone would be mean, but I agree that it could happen. X might tell a *lot* of friends."

Mr. N nodded as if considering. "And social media just makes it easier to spread Y's secret." He looked like he was about to say something more. But instead, he put the first paper down and reached for another.

"Let's hear this one, and see if some different ideas come up."

So here's the situation . . .

Josh gripped the edge of his desk so hard he felt a knuckle crack—those were *his* words! He thought, *Is Mr. N choosing papers at random, or did he pick mine on purpose?*

Mr. N looked up and said, "Everyone should be careful

not to begin sentences with the word *so*. People do this a lot, but it's usually not good writing, or good speaking, either—unless *so* means *therefore*. I'll start again, but I'll leave off *so*."

Here's the situation: Person X has found out something really interesting about Person Y, but X has also learned that Y doesn't want anyone else to know about it, even though the secret isn't about anything bad.

First of all, X might feel confused about this. Because if this information about Y isn't bad, then how come Y wants it to stay a secret? And what if X thinks that the secret is completely awesome and super-interesting, so interesting that X might have told Person Z right away, before X even knew that Y wanted all of it to stay a total secret? Something like that could make this situation more complicated.

Person X would probably hope that Person Y would want to have a talk about everything as soon as possible. That way, Y could explain how come the secret ought to stay a secret, and maybe X would understand the reasons, and do exactly what Y wants.

Or maybe not. It all depends.

Josh felt sweaty and short of breath. His name was on the paper. Had he somehow given away that he was Person X?

Did Mr. N suspect that X had actually told Y's secret to Person Z? He didn't know.

Mr. N *must* see how nervous he looked, though. But any kid whose assignment was being read aloud by a teacher would look that way, right?

Mr. N said, "Any reactions to this writer's ideas?"

Several hands went up, including Vanessa's. Josh began wishing with all his might: *Don't call on Vanessa, don't call on Vanessa, don't call on Vanessa!*

Mr. N said, "Vanessa?"

And then Josh began wishing he could shrink to the size of a squirrel, dive into his backpack, and zip it shut behind him. That wish didn't work either.

"So, I get what the writer is asking about telling Person Z," Vanessa said. "Because your assignment doesn't say *when* X learned that Y didn't want the secret to get out. So X could have told Z, and then found out Y wanted the secret to stay secret."

"True," Mr. N said. "Only watch that *so* word—you just started your sentence with it."

"Oh—sorry." Vanessa smiled and went on. "But also, your assignment didn't give any details about *how* Person X discovered Person Y's secret."

She didn't seem the least bit nervous, and Josh was

amazed. Then he remembered that this was Vanessa the Brave, Vanessa the Wild . . . and sometimes Vanessa the Careless.

Mr. N frowned. "Why would it matter how X found out?"

"Well, if X had sneaked into Y's house and opened a drawer and read a file marked TOP SECRET, wouldn't that be different than if X just noticed something without really trying to—something anybody could have seen?"

Mr. N said, "That's an interesting question. But as it says in the assignment, right now, X *knows* that Y would like this secret to stay a secret. Would it matter how X discovered it?"

Vanessa said, "Yeah, I get that . . . but what if X thinks that Y's secret is like an important news story, something *everybody* ought to know? Because news reporters discover secrets all the time, and then they blast them out to the whole world. Maybe it's like that."

Mr. N said, "But *is* Person X a news reporter?"

"Well, maybe . . . ," she said, "and even if they're not a *real* one . . . X could be *kind of* a reporter, because isn't everybody like a reporter? Regular people take pictures and videos with their phones all the time, and then those can turn into news stories that fly around. Like everyone's always telling us how nothing stays secret anymore."

Josh gave a silent cheer for Vanessa and her logic. He figured she was done talking. She wasn't.

"And besides," she continued, "in the assignment, you said that Y's secret isn't about something bad, so that must mean that it's mostly about something good, right? And why should something that's good have to stay a secret?"

Mr. N got up and walked over to look out the window. He stood there a moment, scratching his hairy cheek. Josh thought Vanessa's question had stumped him.

"It makes sense that if Y's secret isn't about something bad, then it must be about something that's mostly good," he finally said. "And actually, if Y's secret *were* about something bad, then X *should* tell someone. Because that's one way bad things get stopped. That is some of what professional news reporters do."

Now Mr. N turned back to her. "But if this secret is about something good, and if Person Y *still* wants it to stay a secret, then who should be allowed to make that decision: Y or X?"

Now Vanessa was the one who looked stumped. "Well . . . um . . . I'm not sure."

She leaned back in her seat.

Josh was impressed. No one else he knew had ever won an argument with Vanessa.

Mr. N looked around the class. "Anyone with other thoughts about this?"

No hands.

"All right, then please take out your *Elements of Style*—and hold up the books for a quick check. Thank you. Miguel, it's your turn to read aloud. Reminder Eleven and the sentence that follows, please."

Josh found his copy and raised it over his head so Mr. N could look for missing books. This was a stupid routine, and it usually annoyed him. But today it was a relief to move on to something familiar, something safe. Something that didn't have anything to do with secrets and Person X, Y, or Z!

Then Miguel read Reminder 11:

11. Do not explain too much.
It is seldom advisable to tell all.

A shiver ran up Josh's spine. Mr. N wasn't done with secrets after all. In fact, he was sending Person X a message. That message? Don't tell all about *frindle*!

Chapter 8

Equation

As they walked out of Mr. N's classroom, Vanessa whispered, "That was so *weird!*"

Josh whispered back, "Yeah—*bizarro!*"

Vanessa leaned closer and grabbed Josh's arm. "That second assignment he read was *your* homework, right?"

Josh looked over his shoulder. Mr. N was erasing his chalkboard—safely out of earshot. Still, he led Vanessa away from room 113 before answering. "Yeah, it was mine."

Vanessa let out a long breath. "Thought so. When he read that bit about Person Z, I almost lost it! And FYI? It would have been nice to know about that ahead of time."

Josh said, "Sorry—but as far as Mr. N knows, Person X telling Person Z the secret was all a 'what if' thing. And if you're so worried about drawing attention to yourself, how come you raised your hand and started that argument?"

Vanessa made a face. "Okay, maybe I shouldn't have done that."

Josh started to agree. Then something hit him. Something he hadn't thought of before, but that now struck him as *very* important. "You know what? It's not a problem. Even if Mr. N figures out that I'm X and you're Z, it won't matter."

"How do you figure?"

"Think about it! We know his secret, and there's nothing he can do to stop us from telling anyone we want. So *we're* in charge, not him!"

"So?"

"So, last night I was rereading this newspaper article from Mr. N's hometown in New Hampshire," Josh said. "It told how Nick Allen started saying the word *frindle* instead of *pen* at school. There was a picture of his teacher, this lady named Mrs. Granger, and she was *not* having it. It turned into a big battle, and all the kids were on Nick's side."

"Again . . . so?"

"So, what if we get all the kids on *our* side?"

Vanessa frowned. "Sorry. I don't get it. You want us to gang up on Mr. N? What would we even be fighting for?"

Josh knew exactly what he'd fight for. But before he could tell Vanessa his idea, Miguel hurried past on his way to math class. "Josh, come on!" he cried. "You know Mrs. Fusaro gets mad if any of us are late!"

"I'll tell you my idea tonight!" Josh said to Vanessa as he followed Miguel.

"Seriously? You're just going to leave me hanging? Fine. But this idea better be worth the wait."

Josh grinned. "Oh, it is!"

He was five seconds late for math, and his teacher gave him a look as he sat down and fumbled around to find the right workbook page on his laptop. Math had been his favorite subject since kindergarten. He liked how simple functions—addition and subtraction, multiplication and division—paved the way to working out more complex equations. It was the same with computer coding. Master the basics first, and then use that know-how to tackle the more challenging stuff. Anyone who skipped ahead was just asking for trouble.

Mrs. Fusaro was marching her class through a unit on ratios. It was a good thing he grasped the subject, because as

Mrs. Fusaro began writing on the whiteboard, he couldn't focus on the numbers. Today he was more interested in words—something new for him. And one *particular* word was stuck in his head.

How did Nick Allen come up with the word frindle? *And why make it mean pen? Why not key or shoe or book? And how come it's even a noun? Why not an adjective? It could mean . . . loud—a frindle motorcycle, or the frindle explosion. . . . Nah, that doesn't sound right. Adjectives have to sound . . . like adjectives—an* old *frindle, the* shiny *frindle, a* blue *frindle, that* fancy *frindle. It's a weird made-up word, but* frindle *sounds so* real, *plus* goofy *and* strange *all at the same time! And when you say* frindle, *it sounds kind of funny without trying to.* Frindle *is just so . . . so . . .*

With a jolt, Josh sat up straight—and knocked his laptop onto the floor.

Mrs. Fusaro stopped talking, her marker stuck in the middle of an equation on the whiteboard.

She looked down at the laptop. "Broken?"

Josh picked it up and touched the screen. To his relief, it flared to life. "It's working fine. Sorry."

Mrs. Fusaro went back to her equation, and Josh went back to his thoughts. But now he was thinking about Vanessa's question.

"You want us to gang up on Mr. N? What would we even be fighting for?"

It wasn't that Josh wanted to gang up on his teacher. But he did have something worth fighting for. In fact, he had the perfect end goal in mind. It was ambitious, and he couldn't just jump ahead. To achieve it, he had to start with something simple, something basic, just as he did with math and coding.

Josh flicked open a note page on the laptop and tapped out a single line:

frindle = pen

Then he typed a new word underneath this line: *frindy.*

Josh whispered that last word to himself: *frindy . . . frindy . . .*

Frindy sounded like a real adjective—an adjective that meant strange. Or weird. He added to the line so it read:

frindy = funny = weird = odd = goofy = strange

Josh put it into a sentence: *Mr. N gives such frindy assignments!*

He tried another one: *We had a lot of frindy weather last month.*

And then he got creative: *That guy has the frindiest boots I've ever seen—even frindier than Captain America's!*

The more Josh tested the word, the more he liked it. He hoped Vanessa and others would too. In fact, his plan depended on it.

Chapter 9

Making Something Happen

J osh stayed after school on Wednesday for his Python coding club. He wouldn't be able to start homework until after dinner. But before his family sat down to eat, he had just enough time to check the link and reread the assignment for that night:

Homework due Thursday
Choose a place in the world that you know something about but have never visited.

Maybe you have seen this place in a movie or on the internet, or read about it in a book or a blog.

In two or three paragraphs totaling at

least 150 words, describe what it might be like for you to actually arrive at this place for the first time.

Bring your final draft to class tomorrow, written in blue or black ink on lined paper. As usual, neatness counts. And don't forget about this advice from Reminder 18 on page 80 of *The Elements of Style:* "Use figures of speech sparingly."

Mr. N

Josh grinned as he tucked his phone into his pocket and picked up his fork. Use figures of speech sparingly? No problem. He didn't plan to use any. He *was* going to use one special adjective, though.

And he hoped others would too.

During dinner Josh asked his mom, "The other night when I found that old pen of yours, you said *frindle* was kind of a big deal at your school. In what way?"

Josh's sister said, "Frizzle!"

Sophie was almost two, and she hated being left out of anything.

Josh said, "It's *frindle,* Sophie. Can you say *frindle?*"

"Frizzle—*frizzle frizzle frizzle!*"

His mom said, "When the kids started calling pens frindles, most of the teachers thought it was a bother. So it was like a tug-of-war. They wanted us to stop, but we didn't."

"*Stop frizzle!*"

Josh's dad said, "It's *frindle*, Sophie—and by the way, this word didn't catch on at my school up in Sacramento, so I never had the frindle experience. After your mom and I met at college, we were in the library one afternoon, and she asked if she could borrow a frindle, and I had no idea what she was talking about. So I heard the whole story."

Josh looked back at his mom. "Who won the tug-of-war at your school?"

"Well, it didn't turn into some big showdown. It was more like the teachers were the beach, the kids were the ocean, and the waves kept coming. So the teachers finally gave up. The word stuck around for the whole school year and a lot of the next, but by the time I got to the middle of eighth grade, frindles had mostly turned back into pens again. I think it lasted longer with the younger kids, but a year and a half was about it for my group."

"But you remembered it, right? And you kept that frindle."

"*Frizzle!*"

"I remembered because there was something powerful about the whole experience. It made a strong impression on me."

"How come? It's kind of a goofy word, don't you think?"

"Yes, but there was more to it than the word *frindle.*" His mother put down her fork and leaned forward. "It was about all the kids making something happen on our own, making something change."

"Making something change," Josh repeated. "Right. I get that."

"*No!*" Sophie yelled. "*Get frizzle!*"

◼ ☐ ▨ ▨ ☐ ☐ ☐ ▨

Later on, as Josh did his homework, he reread Mr. N's assignment. Then he opened a Messages window on his laptop and sent a text to Vanessa.

> Can we get a message to everyone in Mr. N's class?

> Sure—email or text? I've got a ton . . .

. . .

Hello? You still there?

Sorry—counting. I have emails for 17 in our class, plus there is that big group chat with a few kids in the other sections.

Cool. I have an idea.

Is Person Z feeling brave?

Always.

Rather than messaging, Josh video called to explain his idea.

"Let me get this straight," Vanessa said. "You want everyone in Mr. N's class to use a made-up adjective in tonight's ELA homework? Why?"

"To play a little joke. I think he'll like it."

"It could affect our grade," she pointed out.

"Maybe," Josh admitted. "But then again, Mr. N wants us to write creatively. What's more creative than coming up with our own word?"

Vanessa gave him a look. "This made-up adjective . . . is it *frindle?*"

Josh rolled his eyes. "Of course not. *Frindle* is a noun. Our adjective is *frindy.*"

Vanessa laughed. "Okay, I like it. Now explain the point of this frindy prank."

"It's kind of a test," Josh said. "I want to see how many of Mr. N's students will join in."

"Because . . . ?"

"Because then I'll know if it's worth moving on to step two of my plan."

Then he told her what step two was. And what the ultimate goal of his plan was. Her eyes grew big. "Wow. Here I thought I was the brave one!"

"You are brave—if you agree to help me!"

And, of course, she did.

They worked together on the message. At 7:22, they emailed and texted it to most of the kids in Mr. N's second-period class, and then sent it to all his other students she had contact information for:

•• *FLASH DARE!!!* ••

CAN ***YOU*** USE THE WORD

FRINDY

IN MR. N'S HOMEWORK FOR THURSDAY?

"FRINDY? What's *that*??"

IT JUST MEANS <u>WEIRD</u>, <u>WACKY</u>, <u>STRANGE</u>, <u>ODD</u>!!!

SO . . . GO FOR IT! USE IT!! <u>NOW!!!</u>

<u>OBEY!!!!</u>

[please]

ALSO . . . tell every kid you know who has Mr. N for ELA!

• *FRINDY 4EVER!!!!* •

After sending the message, Josh added some new items to the Frindle Files folder: a photo he had taken of the homemade frindle he had put on Mr. N's desk; a screenshot of Mr. N's assignment about Person Y and Person X; a snapshot of his paper that Mr. N had read aloud in class; and of course, a screenshot of the *frindy* dare they had just sent out. What he wished he had? A picture of Mr. N's face as he had looked at the word *frindle* on that pen!

It was almost bedtime as Josh finished his final draft of

Mr. N's assignment for Thursday—written on lined paper in black ink, neatly. Before he put it into his backpack, he took a picture of it with his phone. His phone and his laptop were synced, so the photo would automatically turn up in his computer's Pictures file—another item for the Frindle Files.

And then he wondered how many other kids would use the word *frindy* in tomorrow's homework . . . or would it be only Vanessa and him?

He hoped not.

Because the word *frindy* was seriously similar to *frindle*—dangerously similar, terrifyingly similar. If enough students used it, it would be like the wave his mother had talked about.

Only this time, Mr. N would be the beach.

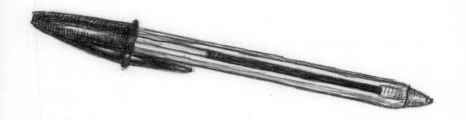

Chapter 10

A Frindy Day

Thursday morning, Mr. N collected the ELA homework, glanced at the top paper, and laughed out loud.

"Allie, you used a word here I haven't seen before." Then he read, "'When I asked for directions to the Eiffel Tower, the man gave me a frindy look.' Does *frindy* mean angry?"

Allie shook her head. "It means strange. Or weird."

"Oh—I see," said Mr. N. "And where did you learn this word?"

Josh wanted to sneak a glance at Vanessa but didn't dare.

Allie said, "I got it from my friends. I guess it's slang."

Mr. N looked back at Allie's paper, and then began

flipping through the other assignments, stopping now and then to read out loud.

"'It was so frindy to be walking up these narrow stairs inside of a giant green statue.' . . . 'Then I found the frindiest part of the whole museum.' . . . 'I had to put on this frindy suit before they let me float toward the space station.' . . . 'I saw these frindy animals called llamas.'"

He laughed again. "It looks like *frindy* is the word of the day, so let's get to know it better."

Mr. N wheeled his chalkboard over beside his desk, picked up a piece of yellow chalk, and began to write.

"It's spelled *f-r-i-n-d-y—frindy,* which rhymes with *windy.* And *frindy* means strange or weird. Who can tell me what part of speech it is?"

Hands went up, and Mr. N said, "Emery?"

"It's an adjective."

"Good, and what does an adjective do . . . Liam?"

"An adjective describes a noun or a pronoun."

"Yes, and what are some different ways adjectives can describe things or people? . . . Rachel?"

"They can tell which, what kind of, or how many."

"Excellent. And which of these jobs does *frindy* do . . . Jack?"

"It tells what kind of."

"Correct. Now, what about that one I read, 'the frindiest part of the whole museum'—who can tell me what's going on there . . . Vanessa?"

Josh tensed up, but Vanessa was calm and clear. "Adjectives can change like that, by adding *e-r* or *e-s-t*. And there are special names for those . . . but I can't remember them."

"Anyone else recall?"

No hands.

"Okay," said Mr. N, "here's the review: When something is *more* frindy than some other thing, then you can add *e-r* to make what's called the comparative form. Except, since *frindy* ends with the letter *y*, first you have to change the *y* to *i* before you add the *e-r*. And if something is the *most* frindy, you can add *e-s-t* to make what's known as the superlative form of the adjective. And again, you change the *y* to *i* before you add the suffix. Now, everyone, please take out a sheet of paper and a pencil, and we'll do a quick review on adjectives, and then we'll see if we can figure out some *frindy* new ways to use this word!"

As Vanessa turned to reach for her backpack, she looked at Josh with her tongue hanging out—as if she were about to throw up.

Josh felt the same way.

But then he began thinking like a programmer—asking

questions and breaking this situation into smaller chunks of information.

When Mr. N first saw the word *frindy,* instead of looking upset or getting mad, he had laughed.

Why—to hide how upset he was? Or did he really think it was funny?

Josh wasn't sure.

Then Mr. N had read more papers and kept smiling.

Why? He didn't seem upset or worried—not a bit. He thought it was actually funny.

And right now, Mr. N was turning *frindy* into a lesson.

Why?

Instantly, Josh understood.

He's trying to kill it! This is word murder . . . death by grammar!

Mr. N was going to grind *frindy* into chalk dust and blow it away with the windy noise of his own talking. Ten more minutes of this, and no kid would ever want to use Josh's made-up word again.

And Mr. N was loving every second of it . . . because he was *not* going to make the mistakes that Nick Allen's teacher had made. This *frindy* thing was too much like what that boy had done years and years ago—but unlike Mrs.

Granger, Mr. N was ready to sideline the word, and the person behind it.

Josh remembered that picture of Mrs. Granger from the newspaper article he'd found online. She'd been wearing a dark skirt and jacket, standing stiff and straight, her gray hair pulled back, her sharp eyes aimed directly at the camera. That lady was tough, *totally* old-school— she was probably why the expression *old-school* had been invented!

Josh felt like the classroom lights suddenly got brighter, and in a moment of dazzling clarity he saw that Mrs. Granger was like an early video game, maybe *Teacher, version 1.0*—a single-purpose program that made it impossible for the user to do anything other than one thing.

But Nick Allen had hacked Mrs. Granger's program and accomplished something completely different! Something great, in fact, that made him famous!

And Mr. N? This guy was an advanced version, a next-next-next-next-generation video game—more like *Teacher, version 8.3*. With his Hawaiian shirts and silly dance moves, he was more user-friendly . . . and he probably thought that *Teacher 8.3* was perfect, unhackable. Turning the tables on Person X and *frindy* had proven that. Right?

Wrong! Because Person X knew something Person Y didn't: the game wasn't over.

And X had pulled a secret lever, opened a hidden door, and dashed up a blazing staircase into a whole new level, a level that wasn't about Mr. N and his *frindle* secret anymore. *This* part of the game was about something bigger, about something happening right now, not twenty years ago.

Today's *frindy* experiment was only a warm-up, like a preview episode on an Xbox at Walmart.

The *real* game was just beginning.

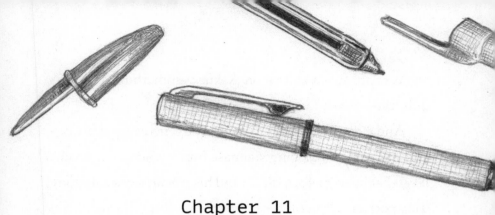

Chapter 11

Hacktivity

On Wednesday morning almost a week later, Mr. N said, "I read a news article last night about a woman in Chicago who learned seven new languages. She said that when she thinks the simplest thought in English, she automatically begins to translate it into all the other languages. Some nights she can't get to sleep because her mind won't stop translating. And *now* she's trying to *forget* all those languages except English! Isn't that one of the *frindiest* things you've ever heard?"

A few kids laughed, and so did Mr. N.

Not Josh. He had to stifle a groan.

Since its introduction the week before, Mr. N had used

frindy during class at least once a day, always with a smile or a chuckle. He had turned the adjective into a big joke.

And even if he hadn't meant to, he'd made Josh, the creator of *frindy,* into a big joke too.

Which is why Josh didn't feel bad about what was going to happen next.

Mr. N said, "Speaking of the English language, the rest of this week we will focus on paragraphs—what they are, how they work, and how to get better at writing them. Please open *The Elements of Style* to Chapter Two, Item Thirteen. First, though, hold up your copies."

Mr. N glanced around the room—and then froze.

Above the waving sea of small paperbacks, lifted extra high for all to see, were four laptops. Josh, Vanessa, Miguel, and Hunter each held one.

Showing the laptops instead of the book? That was step two in Josh's hack of Mr. N's program. He hadn't emailed and texted all Mr. N's students this time, though. There was a chance his scheme could backfire badly, so he'd only contacted his three closest friends. When he explained his plan, they'd jumped on board.

He'd sent a follow-up text to Vanessa, Miguel, and Hunter with a link to a free online version of *The Elements of Style.* They could have downloaded the e-book from the school library. But Josh worried the librarian might inform Mr. N. It felt safer, and smarter, to put the file he'd found on their laptops.

His friends had followed his directions to the letter. And now step two of Josh's plan had been launched.

Mr. N's voice was cold. "I'm sorry to see that some of you are getting check marks today."

It didn't happen often, but Mr. N could do this evil-eye thing—arching his left eyebrow and dipping the right one at the same time. And now the evil eye was on full display, aimed directly at Josh.

Josh raised his hand anyway.

"Yes?"

"I shouldn't get a check mark. You said we had to have *The Elements of Style* with us every day, and I've got mine— here, I'll start reading Item Thirteen!"

Josh jumped to his feet, tapped his laptop screen, and read.

13. *Make the paragraph the unit of composition.*
The paragraph is a convenient unit; it serves all
forms of literary work. As long as it holds together,
a paragraph may be of any length—a single,
short sentence or a passage of great duration.

Josh sat down.

Mr. N reached for his grade book, opened it, then pulled a red marker from the mug on his desk. "A check for Vanessa, a check for Miguel, a check for Hunter, and *two* checks for Josh—one for not having his book, and the other for reading out of turn."

Josh raised his hand again, but Mr. N ignored him and spoke to the class.

"Please open your books to page fifteen, and read all of section thirteen silently at your desks. Underline what you think are the key points, make notes so you can explain why your points are important, and in ten minutes or so we'll have a discussion." Then he said, "Vanessa, Josh, Miguel, Hunter—bring your laptops to my desk."

Josh still had his hand in the air, and Mr. N said, "Yes?"

"I can't do the assignment if you take away my book."

"Your book?" Mr. N held up his copy of *The Elements of Style*. The evil eyebrows were gone, but when he spoke, his voice had an edge to it. "*This* is a book, Mr. Willett. What you have on that machine are bits and bytes programmed to make shapes on a screen. What happens to that book if you remove the electricity or break the screen? What if your machine gets too hot or too cold?"

Josh shifted in his seat but said nothing.

"After I paid for this book," Mr. N went on, "it became mine. I wrote my name in it because I own it. It never needs batteries, and I can keep it my whole life. I can share it with my children or my grandchildren. Yours will be lost to you when you turn *that* in at the end of the school year." He pointed at Josh's laptop.

The whole class was gawking at Josh by then, but he didn't blink. He said, "The only time I ever use that paper book is here in class or for homework. It's just information." Josh held up his laptop again. "I have the same information right here. More, actually, because I can touch or click any word, and *my* copy tells me the definition." He touched the screen. "Like, *exuberance?*—it means 'full of energy, excitement, and cheerfulness.' In *my* book, if I want to find out what it says about adverbs, I type *adverb* in the search field, and I can see everything at once, just like that."

He snapped his fingers.

"In your book, the words are tiny. If I tap here, and then here, the type gets bigger and easier to read. If I misplace or lose my paper book, I have to buy a new one. But if I accidentally delete my e-book from my laptop, I can get the exact same version again. All the textbooks used in the whole school are on a server in the library, ready to download for free."

"And is that what you, Vanessa, Miguel, and Hunter did—download the approved edition from the school library?" Mr. N asked.

Josh lifted his chin. "No. I used technology and found one online. For free. And I texted the link to my friends on another piece of tech: my phone."

The evil eye appeared again, and Josh thought he might have pushed Mr. N too far. He got ready for an explosion.

It didn't come.

"May I see this e-book of yours?" Mr. N asked.

Josh spun his laptop so it faced his teacher.

Mr. N scanned the screen, then nodded. "Thank you, Josh, for sharing that and your opinions. Now we're going to move on with the assignment I've given to the class. And if you four students don't have your own *books* here today, then borrow a copy of *The Elements of Style* from the extras at the back of the room—but instead of underlining key ideas, make all your notes on a sheet of paper. And you may have your computers back . . . at the end of the school day."

Without another word, Josh, Vanessa, Miguel, and Hunter closed their laptops and stacked them on Mr. N's desk, got their borrowed books, sat back down, and began to work.

Josh kept his face calm and serious, but inside he was laughing and hooting.

Yes, he had stopped standing up to Mr. N and handed over his laptop—but not because he was afraid of getting more check marks. Josh had obeyed Mr. N because the events of the past few minutes had unfolded *exactly* the way he had planned.

Mr. N didn't know it yet, but his program had just been hacked.

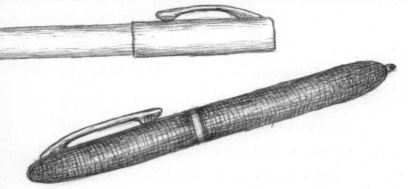

Chapter 12

>>>print ("Hello, Mr. Ortega!")

On this particular Wednesday, Josh was especially glad to be staying late for his coding club. He was also glad that the library was directly across the front hallway from the office.

Right after school, Josh had picked up his laptop from Mr. N's room, then hurried to the library, sat at a table near the windows, and rushed through his first Python exercises with Ms. Hernandez and the group. Now and then, he glanced through the window to the office. He didn't see anything interesting, just the usual kids and staff coming and going. But he was sure something would happen across the hall before coding club ended.

Josh had recruited James Asher to be a spy for him in

Mr. N's last class of the day. James had texted Josh right after sixth period about an intercom call from the school secretary. She had asked if Mr. N could come speak with the principal at four o'clock. Mr. N had said yes, and now Josh had a front-row seat to observe the outcome of the events he had set in motion.

He took his phone from his pocket and thumbed to his flowchart for today's hack on Mr. N.

> 4 kids bring laptops to Mr. N's class and he takes them away for the period

> 4 kids complain to Mr. Ortega about not being allowed to use laptops and an e-book in Mr. N's class

OR

> 4 kids bring laptops to Mr. N's class and he takes them away for the whole day

> 4 missing laptops annoy 6 other teachers teaching 3 other academic subjects

4 kids explain to other teachers how Mr. N
took away laptops as punishment

↓

As many as 6 teachers complain to Mr. Ortega about Mr. N

Josh hadn't been sure if Mr. N would keep their laptops all day, but he was so happy that he had. Complaints to the principal from teachers had gotten quick results—probably quicker than complaints from four kids would have.

At 3:56 p.m., Josh saw Mr. Ortega come out of his office. He went over and spoke to the school secretary, and as he turned around, Mr. N walked in from the hall.

The two men smiled and shook hands, but not the way friends do. They looked so different—the principal wearing a gray suit, white shirt, and tie, and Mr. N in his Hawaiian shirt, shorts, and sandals.

Mr. Ortega held out one arm, inviting Mr. N into his office.

The door closed, and Josh checked the time on his phone—3:57.

Josh tried to imagine the conversation inside the principal's office. There were a lot of possibilities, but they would *have* to talk about the student technology policy at Clara Vista Middle School. Right in the *Student and Parent Handbook* it said, "Every child in grades one through six will be supplied with a laptop. Teachers are expected to guide students in the appropriate and effective use of learning technology in their classrooms so that children will be prepared to use these vital tools in their future studies and careers."

Mr. N had made it clear from the beginning that he believed in the loophole: It was the word *expected* that let him keep laptops and e-books out of his classroom. If he had been *required* . . . well, then he might not have been summoned to Mr. Ortega's office, because he wouldn't have had a choice about allowing tech.

Josh saw the principal's door open, and checked the time: two minutes and seven seconds had passed, maybe the shortest meeting ever.

Mr. N came out alone. There was no goodbye handshake from Mr. Ortega, no smile or wave for the school secretary as Mr. N left the office. He didn't seem upset— more like deep in thought, with his eyes aimed at the floor. Then, just as Mr. N walked out into the hallway, he glanced up.

Josh's stomach dropped and he suddenly felt ill. Had he taken this too far? He almost ducked for cover, but it wouldn't have helped—the library windows stretched from the ceiling almost to the floor. And at 4:00 p.m. on that Wednesday afternoon, they looked at each other—Josh and Mr. N, Person X and Person Y, student and teacher.

Their eyes met only for a second before Mr. N walked on. Josh couldn't tell if his teacher seemed angry or amused.

And suddenly the most basic binary question popped into his head: *Did I win or lose?*

He didn't have the answer because he didn't know what Mr. N and Mr. Ortega had talked about. He tried to focus on his next coding exercise. But he struggled, even though the line he was working on was simple.

Simple. Josh paused and repeated that word to himself—*simple.*

The word triggered a memory: two sentences from "The Zen of Python," a list of nineteen guidelines about writing effective computer code. Ms. Hernandez had shared the list with the club at the start of the year. The two Josh recalled were:

```
Simple is better than complex.
Complex is better than complicated.
```

Thinking about the events of the last nine days, Josh saw how quickly his plan had moved from his simple *frindy* prank to his complex laptop scheme. And now?

Now things seemed like they might get complicated.

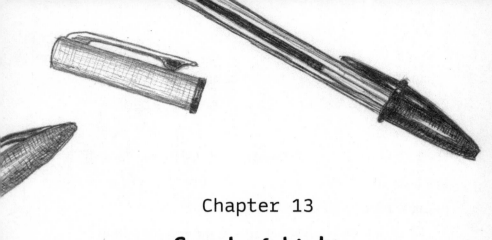

Chapter 13

Speed of Light

When Josh clicked his language arts homework link after school on Wednesday, he got a clearer idea about what had happened during Mr. N's short meeting with the principal.

Announcement

All students are allowed to use their school-issued laptops in class from here on out. In addition, download the free version of *The Elements of Style* from the school library. If you cannot access it from home, Mrs. Krenske will be available to help before and during school on Thursday. All students must also continue to bring the paperback copy of *The Elements of Style* to class each day. *Both the book and the e-book will be needed for work in class and for homework assignments.*

<u>Homework due Friday</u>
Describe in one paragraph the moment when a new student arrives for the first time at a new school. For ideas about how long your paragraph should be, read the paragraph that begins on the third line from the top of page 16 in your paperback copy of *The Elements of Style*. We'll discuss in class tomorrow, and Friday you will turn in your final draft written in blue or black ink on lined paper. As always, neatness counts.
Mr. N

After Josh read the assignment, he dragged a copy of it into the Frindle Files folder. Today's hack seemed like it was part of that story now, because a kid named Nick had hacked Mrs. Granger's program, and now a kid named Josh had hacked Mr. N's program.

Moments later, his phone dinged—a text from Vanessa.

> **RESULT! Laptops in room 113 tomorrow! You DID it!**

Josh smiled and wrote back.

> **Thanks. 😊 Too bad we still have to handwrite homework!**

> **1 step at a time!**

His phone dinged again, Hunter this time.

> **Laptops in class for the WIN!**

Then a text from Marissa Havens arrived. Josh barely knew her. She was in Mr. N's sixth-period class, and her text was copied to a group of thirty-one other kids.

> **Heard you're the guy who got us laptops in Mr. N's class—not bad, Willett**

Mr. N taught three different classes—period two, period four, and period six—seventy-seven kids in all. During the next few minutes Josh got more than twenty texts, each one ending with at least one exclamation point. Most were short, one or two words:

Amazing!

Go Josh!

Yo—sweeeeeet!

Awwwwesome, dude!

Tekkies Rule!

A few of the messages made him laugh:

Looooove my laptop, hate that ancient book!

Screens forever!

Go Team Tech—YAY!

Hunter texted again. He was having trouble accessing the school library website and asked Josh to share his *Elements of Style* link. Josh sent it to him and everyone else in the group.

But the most surprising text came later that night, from Miguel:

> Josh—
>
> You spoke up for all of us! Can you give me an interview for my YouTube channel? 10 minutes, max. Talk at gym tomorrow, OK? Thx!

Miguel's message didn't just surprise Josh—it terrified him.

A video interview? The thought of appearing on You-Tube made his heart pound, made his throat tighten.

He started to tell Miguel he wasn't interested. But a flood of new messages interrupted him. Miguel's text had gone into the group chat. Now everyone in the chain was saying they couldn't wait to see the interview! The messages lit up his small screen like an attack from cyberspace, streaming into his eyes at the speed of light. They kept coming, and the constant dings and vibrations made his phone feel like a frightened hamster squirming in his hand, ready to bite.

Josh shut his phone all the way off, totally dark—something he hadn't done since his birthday back in June.

In the sudden stillness, he tried to enjoy his victory. His plan to get Mr. N to allow laptops in class had worked.

But it had backfired, too, in a way he hadn't seen coming.

Why does everything have to be so complicated? He remembered the line from "Zen": "Complex is better than complicated."

So what comes after complicated?

Complicated is better than . . . what?

Tangled?

Yes.

Muddled?

Yes.

Jumbled?

Again, yes.

Each of these adjectives seemed almost accurate, almost correct.

Josh had a sudden realization. Finding the right word was like writing the right line of code. Once you got it, everything fell into place. He also realized that since his first day of sixth grade, Mr. N had been programming *him*, making him work at his writing—which was why he kept on looking for the right word now.

And when he found it, he was surprised. Because the

best answer to his question was not another adjective. It was a noun.

As Josh whispered the completed sentence, a chill ran down his spine:

Complicated is better than . . . chaos! *If I'm at complicated now, is chaos far behind?*

Chapter 14

On Purpose

Those late-night texts had rattled Josh. Thursday morning, he planned to tell Miguel he didn't want to do the interview. But he didn't. Because suddenly, people were treating him like Luke Skywalker after blowing up the Death Star! Riding on the bus, walking to his locker, during first-period gym, kids were giving him a thumbs-up, slapping him on the back, or lifting a hand for a high five, and saying things like "Hey, Josh, way to go!" or "Nice work!" or "Guess you showed Mr. N who's boss, huh?"

Josh was overwhelmed by the attention—at first. Then he started to enjoy it. And why not? Testing the waters with *frindy,* bringing e-books and laptops instead of the paper copies of *The Elements of Style* to Mr. N's class, having those laptops taken away all day so that other teachers complained to Mr. Ortega—he had planned every step with one goal in mind: to hack Mr. N's program and get tech into the only no-tech zone in the whole school.

And he'd been victorious!

All those uneasy feelings from the night before, all that fear about complications and chaos? Gone. So when Miguel cornered him in gym class and asked if he could interview him sometime that week, Josh said yes. And as gym class ended, Josh imagined that second-period language arts was going to feel like the ultimate victory lap.

His good mood dipped a little when he saw Mr. N standing in the hall outside room 113 with his arms crossed. His teacher greeted each student with a nod rather than his usual wide smile. Josh slipped past when he was looking the other way.

The other kids didn't seem to notice that anything was wrong. They gave Josh high fives and whispered congratulations before taking their seats.

The bell rang, and Mr. N walked in and stood beside his desk.

"Please hold up your *Elements of Style* books. . . . Good.

And now your laptops. . . . Thank you. Did everyone download the e-book from the library?"

At first, no hands went up. Then Charlotte raised hers. "I had trouble accessing the school's book. So I used Josh's link to the e-book instead."

Josh sat up straighter.

"I see." Mr. N seemed extra calm, and all business—no small talk, no smiles, no *frindy* jokes. "Is that what the rest of you did too?"

Everyone murmured yes or nodded.

"I see," Mr. N said again. Josh thought he might get a glance from Mr. N—maybe a raised eyebrow—some small signal to the kid who had helped his fellow students get the e-book they needed for class. It didn't seem like that was going to happen. It seemed like Mr. N was making a special effort to ignore him.

Part of Josh felt sorry to have upset Mr. N—but it was a very small part of him . . . maybe one percent.

Then Mr. N said, "The homework assignment instructed you to read a passage from the paper copy of your book. But did anyone read the same passage from Josh's version too?"

All hands stayed down, and Josh heard Hunter mutter,

"Bad enough I had to read it once. No way I was reading it twice!"

Mr. N nodded. "Well, you're in for a surprise. And not a nice one." Now he did look at Josh.

"Please open your paper copy of *The Elements of Style* to the title page just inside the front cover," he said. "Open your e-book to the same place. Carefully compare the paperback book with the e-book, and whenever the e-book is incorrect in any way—spelling, punctuation, format, anything—write down the error and the page number. In addition to the new homework writing assignment, your second assignment for tomorrow is to submit a list of corrections up to the end of the chapter called 'Elementary Rules of Usage.' And I want you to begin that assignment right now."

Josh blinked. His first thought? *This has to be a joke!*

Josh's second thought was an accusation: *Oh, I get it— this is the same thing he did with* frindy. *Mr. N wants to make us hate using e-books on our laptops, but instead of a grammar lesson, he's using a proofreading lesson—the worst, most boring chore he could think of!*

As Josh pulled out his paperback, he heard his classmates grumbling too. He figured the assignment would take a few minutes at the most. But Mr. N wasn't kidding about the mistakes. Right on page 2, the word *with* was spelled *w-i-i-h*! Quickly scanning the next few pages, he saw goof after goof. It seemed impossible, but there they were, staring at him from his own screen.

Josh glanced up to see his teacher smiling at him— Mr. N must have watched him as he'd spotted those mistakes. He dropped his gaze back to his screen and asked himself a nonbinary question: How did Mr. N know the free e-book had so many errors?

The answer came to him immediately. *I showed him a page on my laptop yesterday. He must have spotted a mistake, memorized the file name, and then read the same e-book.*

Then he remembered Mr. N's note about seeing Mrs. Krenske. Did he suspect students would have trouble downloading the library's e-book? Did he also suspect that no one would ask the librarian for help? No offense to Mrs. Krenske, but no sixth grader Josh knew would get to school early or ask the librarian, not if they had a solution to their problem at their fingertips. Which they did—Josh's link.

He let me think I was a hero.

Josh didn't feel angry—just embarrassed that Mr. N had outsmarted him so easily. Again.

He glanced at Vanessa. She was staring at her screen, her nose wrinkled, highlighting mistakes. Josh could guess what she'd have to say—*Nice work, genius!* or maybe *Got any more bright ideas?* All those kids this morning who had treated him like he was Luke Skywalker and Han Solo rolled into one? How were *they* going to feel about this?

Josh felt like he deserved whatever insults Vanessa wanted to dish out. And the other kids probably hated him—first *frindy,* and now this.

He moved his cursor to the next error and clicked. All around him, other fingers tapped on keyboards too.

And just like that, his embarrassment washed away, and he smiled to himself. *Mr. N might have won the battle. But thanks to me, we have laptops—so we won the war!*

For about thirty seconds Josh felt so strong and victorious that being forced to hunt for all the incredibly careless mistakes in the e-book was almost fun.

Then Mr. N chuckled. It sounded just like when he had laughed at the word *frindy.* Josh took a careful look at him, sitting there at his desk in his rumpled Hawaiian shirt and his sagging socks, scratching the stubble on his cheek as he smiled at his laptop. He looked completely relaxed, as if he didn't have a care in the world and everything was just as it should be.

Hang on. I beat him. So why is he laughing?

Then it hit him like an earthquake. *What if Mr. N has*

something else up his sleeve? What if that something makes me look bad—again?

He didn't like that possibility. At all.

He raised his hand and waited until Mr. N noticed him. "Yes, Josh?"

"When I showed you the page from the e-book on my laptop yesterday . . . did you see it had mistakes?"

Mr. N raised his eyebrows at the sharp challenge in Josh's voice. The other students looked up.

Mr. N said, "As a matter of fact, I did."

"Why didn't you tell us about it?"

The whole room tensed up, as if every kid had sucked in a breath and held it.

Mr. N stood up and started pacing. "It's a fair question. I didn't tell you about the e-book mistakes because it's good when people learn things for themselves. Explore things for themselves. Question and wonder and research for themselves. So, yes. I could have told you."

Mr. N stopped pacing right in front of Josh's desk. "And you could have looked at the e-book carefully and seen the mistakes yourself, and then we probably would not be having this discussion. And you and your classmates wouldn't be doing the proofreading assignment." He looked around the room. "Are there any other questions?"

None—especially not from Josh.

"All right," Mr. N said. "Please get back to work."

And that's what Josh did.

His face felt warm, and he knew he was blushing.

To fight the embarrassment, he put himself into mindless robot mode, even using a robot voice inside his head: *Find a mistake, make a note. Find a mistake, make a note. Find a mistake . . .*

But deep inside, Josh knew that everything Mr. N had said to him was completely logical and totally true. Josh had been careless—and his classmates were paying the price.

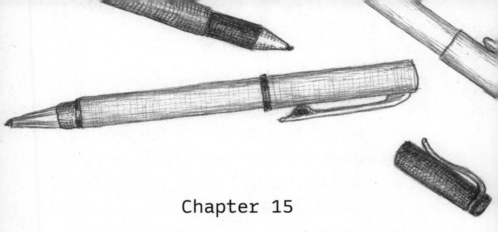

Chapter 15

Explorers . . . and Pirates

"**G**o ahead, say it."

Josh and Vanessa stood in the hall after walking in silence all the way to his math classroom.

"Say what?" she asked, her eyes wide and innocent.

"How none of this would have happened if I'd taken the time to check that e-book before sharing the link with everyone. And if I hadn't kept trying to turn everything into a giant game of Outsmart the Teacher."

"Why, *Joshua*! What in the world do you mean? I would *never* say those things to you! Because, like, why would I bother when you're so good at saying them yourself?"

Josh snorted. "Yeah, why would you bother?"

"But I'll tell you something else. You *did* outsmart the

teacher. Or do you have another explanation for why we were all using laptops in his class just now?"

She went on. "Plus, all that stuff Mr. N said about questioning and exploring and researching things for ourselves? I almost jumped up and yelled out everything you've found out about him—by questioning and exploring and researching! And if telling him what you'd discovered meant revealing his secret to everyone in class, well, sorry, Mr. Secret Frindle Dude!"

For half a second, Josh wanted to say, *Yeah, it'd serve him right!*

But instead he said, "We should probably just forget about that frindle stuff."

"What? Why?"

"Because it's his business, not ours."

Vanessa stuck out her chin. "*You* can do whatever you want. *I'm* going to go whack at that piñata until it splits wide open!"

Josh shook his head. "But Mr. N was right. I stood up yesterday and told the whole class how great the e-book is, how it's so much better and everything, and I hadn't even looked at it—not until I read that part out loud."

"Oh, all right!" Vanessa said. "But, like . . . can we at

least go and *talk* to him? About you-know-what? I promise, I can be all friendly and happy."

Josh shrugged. "What's the point? He doesn't want anyone to know, so why make him go there? Even bringing it up might make him think I want to get back at him or something. And I don't—I really don't."

"Arrrgh," Vanessa growled. And then she sighed. "I guess you're right—but what about the whole changing-his-name thing? Aren't you just dying to *know*? I mean, just for ourselves?"

Josh hesitated. Because Vanessa was right—he was dying to know. "Mr. N did just lecture us about learning things on our own," he said. "So I suppose we could learn about him. *On our own."*

"Yes! Boom!" Vanessa pretended to swing a bat at an imaginary piñata. Laughing, she hurried down the hallway to her next class.

Josh ducked into Mrs. Fusaro's with seconds to spare before being late. He used those seconds to tap out a list:

Frindle

Nicholas Allen

Missing Eight Years

He added a question mark after each line. And he made a promise to himself: if the information was out there, he would track it down.

⬛◻⬛▨　▨◻⬛▨

After school, Miguel cornered Josh at his locker. "So when do you want to do that interview? I have tons of follow-ers from school who'd love to hear the story behind the laptops!"

Josh gulped. He'd forgotten all about Miguel's YouTube channel. Being interviewed about outsmarting Mr. N had seemed like a great idea just two periods ago. Now, though, he wasn't sure he wanted everyone to know he'd shared an e-book full of mistakes with most of Mr. N's students.

"I have coding club," Josh said. "I'll text you about it tonight if I have time."

Miguel gave him a thumbs-up and headed off to the buses. Josh gathered his things and went to the library. He finished his coding work early and used the rest of the time to search for mistakes in the *Elements of Style* download.

Mr. N had told them to proofread the first part of the book. But once Josh got going, it was like eating potato chips: he didn't want to stop. If David Ling hadn't poked his shoulder as he was walking to the printer, Ms. Hernandez might have found Josh hours later, sitting in his seat, hunched over his screen, looking for the next missing comma, the next misspelled word, the next ruined format. It was strangely satisfying, almost like a treasure hunt.

As he proofread for errors, Josh couldn't help reading the book—something he had not really done before. On the first day of school Mr. N had told them that *The Elements of Style* had originally been a college textbook, and he explained that they would use it mostly for reference, not as a book to sit and read.

Midway through the second chapter, a block of text jumped out at him.

17. Omit needless words.

Vigorous writing is concise. A sentence should contain no unnecessary words, a paragraph no unnecessary sentences, for the same reason that a drawing should have no unnecessary lines and a machine no unnecessary parts.

"Omit needless words." Such a simple idea—almost binary! And Josh thought he'd heard it before, except he felt sure he would have remembered if someone had read that sentence aloud in class.

Still, it seemed so familiar—and then the connection hit him.

He pulled up "The Zen of Python" and reread the list. For the first time, he was struck by how some ideas seemed exactly like what he had just read in *The Elements of Style*.

He immediately spotted a good match for "Omit needless words."

```
Sparse is better than dense.
```

The next one matched too—and it was even simpler:

```
Readability counts.
```

And then something else struck him.

Mr. N is into The Elements of Style *the same way I'm into "The Zen of Python." No wonder he's upset about the e-book. If someone messed up "Zen," I'd be angry too!*

He couldn't believe it. The kind of writing Mr. N and the authors of *The Elements of Style* taught was a lot like coding. Keep it simple and straightforward, follow the rules, and you'll get good results.

Mr. N has been showing me how to build code in English,

and what have I been doing? Hacking his program—and being a complete jerk!

"Lost in 'Zen,' Josh?"

Josh glanced up to see Ms. Hernandez reading over his shoulder and smiling.

"I'll never forget the person who introduced me to 'Zen' and to coding," she said. "He was a computer whiz *and* a one-of-a-kind teacher."

Ms. Hernandez was a code analyst for an internet security company. She worked from home and volunteered a few afternoons a week as a coding tutor at the middle school. Josh had a thought: Who better to ask about a messed-up e-book than her?

"Ms. Hernandez? Do you know why an e-book would have tons of spelling and formatting errors and stuff?"

"It depends," she said. "If the e-book is a digital original, meaning it doesn't appear in any other form, then whoever wrote it could have made the mistakes."

"No, it was a real book first. This book, actually." Josh pulled out his paperback to show her. "And this is the e-book."

He closed "Zen" and sat back so she could see *The Elements of Style* on his screen.

"Yikes," she said. "I spot three errors on this page alone! I can't be sure . . . but my best guess is this was pirated."

"Pirated?"

"Someone scanned the real book and used a software program to convert it to digital format. That's legal if the publisher or author agreed to it. But it's illegal—'pirated'— if someone did it without permission. And scanning quickly introduces errors that pirates don't bother to correct. Sometimes they leave lots of errors, like in this book."

She paused, a troubled look on her face. "Mistakes might not be the only problem here, though."

"What do you mean?"

"People who pirate books sometimes piggyback viruses within the links."

Josh's eyes widened. Computer viruses were bad news. They could wipe out files, corrupt the whole system—or worse!

All the school computers came loaded with an antivirus program. The software was good. But even the best programs didn't catch everything.

Ms. Hernandez said, "Let's do a virus scan on your computer now, just to be safe."

Heart pounding, Josh pulled up the program and tapped start. A colorful wheel appeared on the screen and began to tick down the program's progress. Seconds passed. A minute.

Josh's mind was spinning faster than the wheel. If the e-book had a virus, his laptop could be infected. And if his laptop was infected—he swallowed hard—then Vanessa's, and Miguel's, and Hunter's, and the computers of every student who had accessed his link could be too.

He'd thought he was a hero for sharing his version of the e-book. But what if he'd unleashed chaos?

Chapter 16

Perfect

The laptop chimed. The wheel disappeared. In its place was a message from the program:

Congratulations! You are virus-free!

Josh let out a huge sigh. Ms. Hernandez patted his shoulder. "That was lucky. But, Josh, be sure to run a scan at least once a week. And stick to downloading e-books from reliable sources, like the school library, okay?"

"Okay."

Josh thought about his near miss as he packed up his laptop. He thought about it all through dinner that night too. He sent a message to Vanessa and his classmates. They were a little annoyed but, thankfully, virus-free. Josh had been terrified until he knew everything was okay. Then he was relieved.

Now? Now he was angry. With himself for being so stupid. But also with whoever had pirated the book.

I can't believe people do that kind of thing! He pushed open the door to his room, then stopped short. Sophie was climbing his chair to get onto his desk!

"Sophie! No!"

"Frizzle!" She grabbed for something. Her pudgy little hand hit a pile of books. They toppled to the floor.

Sophie would have toppled too if Josh hadn't grabbed her. "Careful there, kiddo! You almost fell!"

She wriggled in his arms and reached toward the desk again. "Frizzle! Have frizzle!"

Josh knew better than to give his little sister a pen. He put her down and handed her their dad's old calculator instead.

"Frizzle, frizzle, frizzle!" Sophie toddled out of the room, pushing the calculator buttons to make the little screen light up with numbers.

Josh started stacking the books back on his desk. They were his favorite paperbacks, the ones his parents used to read to him before bed. He hadn't looked at any of them for a long time. But he remembered how great it had been to burrow under the covers and listen to the stories.

The cover art of one book caught his eye. Its title, *Charlotte's Web*, was draped in spiderwebs. A spider dangled on her silk string in front of a little girl hugging a pig. And below the artwork was the author's name: E. B. White.

E. B. White . . . Where have I heard that name before?

He racked his brain but couldn't come up with the answer—until he sat down to do his homework. When he pulled out his paperback copy of *The Elements of Style*, there it was: Written by William Strunk Jr. . . . and E. B. White!

"No way!" He looked from one book to the other. And asked himself a binary question: Did the same E. B. White write both? YES or NO?

A quick online search provided the answer: YES. William Strunk Jr., a professor of English literature, had written the original book in 1918. E. B. White expanded it in 1959—seven years after he wrote *Charlotte's Web*. And according to the website, White had once been in Professor Strunk's class!

Josh tried to imagine himself working on a book Mr. N had written. He shook his head. The thought was too weird.

He flipped open *Charlotte's Web* to the title page. At

some point, he'd written his name there. He grinned—he still had the same scrunchy handwriting.

Suddenly, something Mr. N had said in class came back to him: *"I wrote my name in it. . . . I can share it with my children or my grandchildren."*

Josh didn't have kids or grandkids. But he did have a little sister. He doubted he'd ever pass *The Elements of Style* on to Sophie . . . but *Charlotte's Web*? That he could see doing.

Maybe he'd even read the paperback aloud to her, just as his parents had done. She was too young now, but that was okay—he found *he* wanted to reread it. He put the book on his nightstand, then pulled out his laptop.

His list of e-book errors fluttered out, and the anger he'd felt earlier surged back. But now it was different. More personal, somehow. Because whoever had pirated *The Elements of Style* hadn't just pirated a book. That person had also pirated E. B. White. Not the actual man, of course—White had died years ago.

But White's name was on that awful e-book. That didn't seem right. In fact, it seemed really, really wrong.

And Josh decided he was going to do something about it. It was time for a new plan.

Chapter 17

The Big Screen

Josh didn't know what it was about the school bus. The laughing and talking, the lurching starts and stops, the roaring engine and squealing brakes, the clattering doors— the bus hardly seemed like a good place to think. But looking out the window, or just staring at the floor mats, sometimes Josh felt like his mind became an island, a tiny spot of stillness in a sea of motion and noise. And once in a while, an idea would swoop down like a seagull and make a graceful landing.

And the idea that landed on this particular Friday afternoon demanded action. He sent a quick text to Vanessa.

Let's find the pirate!

Huh??

Sorry. Forgot you don't know. The mistakes in Elements are because someone pirated the book. Let's find him!

Or her. The pirate could be a her.

Sure sure. Let's find her! We just need to do something.

And will this something involve . . . algorithms??

I AM SERIOUS

OK OK. Sorry.

Are you in?

Of course I'm in!

Good. Come over tomorrow?

Maybe 1:00?

OR you come here and bring your bike? We can ride Canyon Park THEN make a plan.

Sure. Tomorrow at 1, your house.

Cool.

The Canyon Park trail was a nine-mile loop of mostly smooth gravel, and Vanessa had ridden it at least a dozen times. Helmet, gloves, sunglasses, and twenty-seven gears seemed to turn her into a NASCAR driver, and the moment her dad lifted her bike down from the back of his pickup, she was off.

She yelled over her shoulder to Josh, "I'll wait for you at the shelter up along the ridge!"

Her dad called, "Take it easy," but she was already hidden by the low manzanitas beyond the trailhead.

He said to Josh, "Remind her that I'm waiting here in the lot, okay? And call me if there are any problems."

"Will do," Josh said. "See you soon."

This was the fourth time Josh had biked this trail with Vanessa. Actually, it was always biking *behind* Vanessa, never with her. Which didn't bother him at all. He liked setting his own pace, both uphill and down—especially down.

The climb to the ridge wasn't very steep, but Josh put his bike into its lowest gear anyway. For a kid who spent a lot of his time tapping a keyboard, he was in decent shape, but he wasn't trying to set any speed records today.

The uphill side was his favorite part of this trail. He liked the steadiness of the effort, the interlocking rhythm of his legs and his breathing. It was nearly automatic, which left his mind free to wander.

Josh had just started to review the long list of built-in Python functions he was trying to memorize, when a man's voice called, "On your left!"

A bike hauling a child trailer zipped by, and Josh swerved right and then glanced up, annoyed at the interruption. He would have dropped right back into his functions review, but two things about the rider caught his attention: the red hair poking out from under his bike helmet, and the Hawaiian shirt.

Mr. N? Nah, couldn't be! But . . . he does ride a bike to school a lot, and he also has a kid.

Josh shifted to a higher gear and picked up his pace. If he could keep close enough on the climb, he'd have a chance to catch up when they both got to the level stretch along the ridge. And then he'd see.

Whoever the guy was, he was a strong climber. Josh was gasping as he reached the ridge, and the trailer behind the other bike was a yellow dot in the distance, pulling around a bend. So Josh slowed way down, grabbed his water bottle from its clip, and had a long drink.

About five minutes later, he took the turnout toward the shelter, and when Vanessa came into view, there was Mr. N standing beside her, holding a toddler on one hip.

"Hi, Josh! Vanessa told me it must have been you that I passed back there. This is my daughter, Lilly. Can you say hello to Josh?"

The girl shook her head and turned away. She had her dad's red hair and blue eyes.

"She's not usually this shy," he said.

Mr. N set her on her feet, then held her hand and took the path toward the guardrail behind the shelter. "Let's go look at the big screen, okay?"

Vanessa and Josh leaned their bikes against a picnic table and followed.

The view beyond the railing always made Josh dizzy. The land dropped down and away, and each time Josh had stood here, he'd felt sure that the Spanish-speaking settlers who named the town might have stood in the same spot and said those very words: "Clara vista!" To the northwest, the edge of the Los Angeles basin rose up, shrouded by smog. But straight westward there was a clear view all the way to the Pacific.

Vanessa said, "How come you called this the big screen?"

Mr. N smiled and pointed at his daughter. "We've been coming up this trail at least once a month since she was a year old, and one day when we stopped here and looked out, she spread her arms wide and said, 'Big screen!' I took a picture of the view with my phone, and I showed it to her at home that night. But she pushed it away and said, 'No! *Big* screen!'"

Vanessa laughed. "I *love* that!"

"Me too," he said. Then he turned to his daughter. "Lilly, we need to go back to the bike and ride home now. Walk or carry?"

She lifted her arms and said, "Carry," and Mr. N picked her up.

As Josh walked beside them on the path, Mr. N glanced over and said, "Vanessa said there's something you've been dying to ask me. What's on your mind?"

Josh shot her a look, but she avoided his eyes and kept trying to get Lilly to smile.

"Um, yeah," he said to Mr. N, "that's right. I—I wanted to ask you . . . I mean, this might be kind of personal. . . ."

The sun hit his face, and for a second Josh almost asked about *frindle*. "Umm, how come you like Hawaiian shirts so much?"

It was a brilliant save, and Josh saw Vanessa smile, still avoiding eye contact.

Mr. N laughed, and that made his daughter laugh too. "My wife and I went to Hawaii right after we got married, and I came home with three outrageous shirts. I guess I wore them often enough to make people notice, and ever since then, I've gotten a few more each year as gifts from our friends and family. So I've got this self-renewing supply of free, comfortable shirts, plus I like how bright they are— and Lilly loves them. If she sees someone else wearing one, she says, 'It's a Daddy shirt!' "

Back at the shelter Mr. N helped his daughter into the carrier and buckled her harness.

He straightened up and gave them a big smile. "It was great to run into you two today—maybe it'll happen again."

"Yeah," Josh said, "out here on the big screen! See you Monday, Mr. N."

Vanessa waved. "Bye-bye, Lilly!"

Mr. N said, "Have a safe ride down," and then pushed off toward the main path.

As he disappeared, Josh spun toward Vanessa.

"You are *unbelievable!*"

She pretended to be surprised. "*What?* What are you talking about?"

"Very funny! There was something I was 'dying to ask' him?"

"Oh, that! *Actually,* I wondered if he might have any ideas about finding the e-book pirate. Or have you got that all figured out already?"

Before he could answer, she jumped on her bike and took off with a spurt of gravel.

"See you at the parking lot!"

He almost yelled something more, but decided to save his breath. Besides, he wasn't mad, not really. She must have known he wouldn't let himself be pushed into asking about the frindle stuff, and she had been right.

And knowing about the shirts? Kind of fun.

The downhill trail took less muscle but more concentration. Josh had learned the hard way that gravity was not his friend. Speed built up quickly, and unless he kept his front and rear brakes in perfect balance, it was easy to skid out—and he didn't want to spend the rest of the day picking bits of rock out of his legs and arms. He rode extra slowly, and not just for safety. He also wanted time to think.

Josh remembered the only other time he'd come face to face with a teacher outside of school. He and his dad had gone to an all-electric go-kart track over the weekend. After a couple of races they went to the snack bar and Josh saw his third-grade teacher, Ms. Addison, sitting at the next table—except he almost didn't recognize her.

At school she was always soft-spoken, always wore tan pants with a shirt or sweater, always had straight blond hair hanging down to her chin. The lady in the next booth was wearing a black leather jacket over a long red shirt and bright blue tights, and she had deep pink hair spiked out all over her head. And she was *loud,* laughing and joking with the guy across the table from her.

And then she had noticed the kid at the next table, staring at her.

Josh had given a little wave. "Hi, Ms. Addison!"

She had blushed as pink as her hair. "Oh—Josh! Hi!" Then she stood up and came to his table and awkwardly shook hands with his dad, and even more awkwardly introduced her friend, Walter. Soon after, they had left.

A binary question had gradually formed in Josh's mind back then: *Which is the real Ms. Addison:* PINK HAIR *or* BLOND HAIR? Of course, now he understood how a person can look or act differently in different settings and still be the same person, still be real.

But with Mr. N today? He liked how the person biking in the hills with his daughter had seemed *exactly* like the person in his classroom at school: same smile, same voice, same laugh—even the same shirt!

Why did Vanessa think Mr. N, the most antitech person he'd ever known, would have a clue about pirated e-books? And if he did, wouldn't he have said something in class—or at least to Josh, especially if he suspected a virus might be attached to the link?

No, Mr. N wouldn't be any help in tracking down the pirate. That much Josh was sure of.

As he rolled past the eighth mile marker, Josh glanced down at the tire marks Mr. N and Vanessa had left in the dirt. The bikers were long gone, but evidence that they'd been there remained.

Josh braked to a stop as an idea jumped into his mind.

What if the pirate left a trail behind too? Could I trace that trail back to the source and find him—or her?

Excited, he started biking again, faster now. Near the parking lot, he put on a burst of speed. He pulled up beside the pickup and hopped off.

He couldn't wait to talk to Vanessa.

Chapter 18

A Call for Help

"So, what's this great pirate-catching plan and how can I help?"

Josh and Vanessa sat on the couch in her family room. Josh pulled his laptop out of his backpack and clicked on the e-book.

"I was thinking the pirate might have left evidence, like digital bread crumbs, that we could trace back to him. Or her."

She laughed. "Okay, Hansel. How do we find those crumbs?"

"I'm not sure," Josh admitted. "I guess we just start looking."

For the next half hour, they explored every page of the

e-book. And they found exactly . . . nothing. If the pirate had left any clues, they were too well hidden for a pair of sixth graders to find.

"So much for that." Vanessa clicked the e-book closed and flopped back onto the couch.

"You're giving up?" Josh asked.

"It's a dead end!"

"Or maybe we just don't know what to look for or where to look for it!"

"So who does?"

"I could ask Ms. Hernandez for help after school on Monday," Josh said.

Vanessa punched him lightly in the arm. "You couldn't have thought of that half an hour ago?"

She got up to get chips and salsa. While she was in the kitchen, he received a text from Miguel.

Hey, Josh! You free for that interview now?

Josh started to type back that he was busy. Then he remembered what Miguel had said about having tons of followers. Could one of those followers know how to track down the pirate? It was worth a shot.

Miguel lived a few streets over from Vanessa's house. When Vanessa found out what was going on, she insisted on going too. They biked to Miguel's house together.

Miguel led them to a shed in his backyard. "Welcome to my studio," he said, sweeping an arm to invite them inside.

Josh was impressed. The shed was small but set up like a talk show, with two chairs facing one another, a little table with a leafy potted plant, and a tripod for Miguel's phone.

"Nothing fancy," Miguel said. "But it gets the job done."

Vanessa stood behind the tripod. Josh sat in one of the chairs and put his backpack on the floor, out of sight. Miguel set his phone on the tripod. And suddenly, Josh got nervous.

"So, how does this work?" he asked.

"I ask you some questions. You answer them. We talk. And then I edit the video to take out any bad or boring parts."

That made Josh feel a little better.

Miguel pushed the record button on his phone, then sat in the other chair, faced the camera, and grinned.

"Welcome back, loyal viewers! I'm Miguel, and today I'll be talking with Josh Willett."

Josh gave an awkward wave and nearly knocked over the plant. Vanessa smothered a laugh with her hands.

Miguel continued as if nothing had happened. "Many of you know Josh as the mastermind who got a certain ELA teacher to allow laptops in his classroom." He turned to Josh. "Tell us how that came about, Josh."

"Actually, Miguel, I'd like to talk about something else. If that's okay? It's connected to the laptops. Sort of."

Miguel looked mystified, but nodded.

Josh turned to the camera. "It has to do with a terrible e-book, *The Elements of Style*."

Miguel cleared his throat. "*The Elements of Style*? You sure that's what you want to talk about?"

"I'm sure. But not just that." Josh rummaged in his backpack and pulled out his copy of *Charlotte's Web*. "You ever read this book, Miguel?"

Miguel took the book. "Sure, a long time ago. It's about a pig named Wilbur and a spider named Charlotte who saves his life by writing words about him in her web, right?" He smiled. "I liked it."

"Me too." In fact, Josh had reread the whole thing the night before. He couldn't put it down. The story, the characters, the smart, funny writing—all of it was at least ten times better than he remembered. The ending was still rough, but it was a lot better the second time.

"But what does that book have to do with the e-book?" Miguel asked.

"E. B. White, the man who wrote *Charlotte's Web*, also helped write *The Elements of Style*. That e-book link I sent everyone? It's for a pirated version of the original— that means someone made the e-book without permission, which is illegal. And if that's not bad enough, whoever did it didn't even bother proofreading it for errors!" Josh spread his hands out wide. "I hate knowing that E. B. White, the man who created Wilbur and Charlotte and all the other animals in that book, is connected in any way to a pirated e-book with loads of mistakes."

"I get that," Miguel said, nodding. "But what can we do? The e-book is out there for anyone to download."

"But what if it wasn't?" Josh said. "What if we could track down the pirate . . . and force him or her to remove the e-book forever?"

Miguel frowned. "Is that possible?"

"I don't know," Josh admitted. "But I'm hoping one of your viewers does. And that that viewer will get in touch with me, and soon."

Miguel faced the camera again. "You heard him, folks. If you have an idea to share with Josh about taking down a pirate, post it in the comments section below. And don't forget to like this video and subscribe to my channel!"

Miguel got up and turned off his phone. "Well," he said, "that's not quite the interview I expected. It was pretty interesting, though. And speaking of interesting . . ."

He picked up *Charlotte's Web* from the table where Josh had put it. "Can I borrow this?"

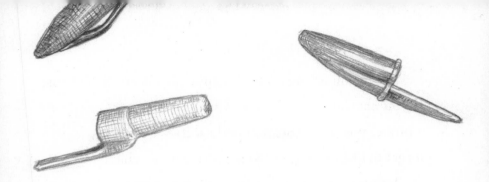

Chapter 19

The Quest / Sounding an Alarm

Vanessa and Josh biked back to Vanessa's house together. While they waited for Josh's mom to pick him up, Vanessa said, "Even if your interview doesn't end up helping, there is something we can do."

"What?"

"Delete that corrupted e-book from our devices and forget about it—and enjoy the good old paperback. *Maybe* download the real one from the library. And anyway, that bike ride was fun, right? Seeing Mr. N and everything?"

Josh nodded. "Yeah, that was great. And you're probably right. Might be time to hit delete. Though I'd rather delete the e-book from everywhere, not just my laptop!"

His mom arrived, and they got his bike bungeed into the trunk.

"See you at school," Vanessa said.

"Yup, see you. And thanks."

Josh told his mom a little about their bike ride, and then sat silently the rest of the way home. His mom thought he was quiet because he was tired, but there was more to it than that.

Josh couldn't figure out why the e-book felt so important to him. The logical thing was to do what Vanessa had said—delete the whole mess and move on.

But deleting it from his laptop would not solve the problem. The errors would live on and on, whether *he* was looking at them or not.

■□■■ ■□□■

That night, he was working on a line of code when a memory tugged at his mind. He opened his old friend "The Zen of Python."

Halfway down the list of sayings, Josh saw what he was looking for.

```
Errors should never pass silently.
Unless explicitly silenced.
```

That e-book was *stuffed* with errors. And letting them pass without making some noise, without sounding an alarm? It was like betraying everything that good programming ought to be—and everything Josh wanted to stand for. To him, a badly written program was an insult, an attack on intelligence and usefulness, a waste of time and energy and thought. And that lousy e-book felt exactly the same to him—insulting, and just plain wrong.

Two days ago he hadn't known about those mistakes. But now that he knew, if he did nothing, from this moment on, they would always be partly *his* fault.

Letting those mess-ups slide without a big, noisy fight? Not an option.

As he climbed into bed, Josh made a promise to himself: *I am going to do whatever I can to silence those errors and delete them from the* universe!

Instantly, he felt silly. Why make a big, dramatic promise and get all worked up about this, when almost no one else cared?

But just as quickly, Josh thought, *A promise is a promise, and I need to keep this one—even though I only made it to myself. . . . No, especially because I made it to myself!*

Josh didn't care if he ended up being alone on his quest. But Sunday morning, he discovered he had an ally—an ally with a mysterious name.

Josh was eating breakfast when Miguel called.

"Pull up your interview on my YouTube page," he said. "And check out the seventh comment."

Josh did as Miguel instructed. He didn't start the video, though. He'd watched it the night before. Seeing himself on-screen once was one time too many, especially since Miguel hadn't edited out the moment he almost knocked over the plant.

He scrolled through the comments under the video until he came to the seventh one. The person who posted it wrote:

Try searching the domain name registration. Then look for the registrant's email address.

The comment was signed "Charlotte's Friend."

"Charlotte's Friend? Who's that?" Josh asked.

"Gotta be someone from school. Most of my followers are students," Miguel answered.

While they were talking, a new comment appeared.

Let me know if I can help!

The poster's name was Marissa H—Marissa Havens. Josh picked out the names of other students, too, even those who didn't use their real names, like Hunter, who went by Ima Hunter.

But who was Charlotte's Friend? An actual friend of Josh's classmate Charlotte? Or did the poster mean Charlotte the spider from *Charlotte's Web*?

Either way, the comment was the only practical advice anyone had offered. The only trouble was, he didn't know how to search for domain name registrations—or even if he should. The near miss with the virus had made him a lot more cautious. And what was he supposed to do with the registrant's email address, if he even found it?

"I'll ask Ms. Hernandez about this stuff at coding club," he told Miguel. "Keep your fingers crossed!"

They ended the call, and Josh clicked off the YouTube page. He was about to shut his laptop when his eyes fell on the Frindle Files.

For some reason, he hadn't told Vanessa about them. Now he didn't have a reason to. With a sigh, he dragged the file to the trash can icon.

But the very next night, he dragged it right back out again. Because he'd found out something unbelievable about Mr. N. Something that belonged in the Frindle Files.

Chapter 20

Surprise

Hurrying past the office after school on Monday, Josh looked through the library windows and saw what he'd been hoping for. So far the day had been like any other. Nothing unusual. Nothing unexpected. But now, back at the table where his coding group met, Ms. Hernandez was bent over the keyboard of her laptop.

As Josh arrived at the table, she kept tapping, barely glancing up.

"How's it going?" she asked. "You make any progress on your game structure?"

"None," he said. "Been working on a different puzzle, a *harder* one. One I hope you can help me with."

Ms. Hernandez stopped typing. "So long as it's a coding problem, I'm sure I can." Josh was sure too.

"Actually," he said, "it's about that *Elements of Style* e-book I showed you last week. You know, the pirated one with all the mistakes?"

She wrinkled her nose. "I remember. What about it?"

Josh opened his laptop, pulled up his YouTube interview, and hit play. She raised her eyebrows but watched the whole video. Josh cringed at the plant part and was grateful when she didn't laugh. When the video ended, he scrolled down and pointed to the seventh comment.

"Ah," she said after she read it. "You want to know how to search for a domain registrant."

"Yes! Can you help me?"

To his disappointment, she shook her head. "I'm sorry, Josh, but I'm not the right person to guide you through that. There is someone here at school who might be able to, though."

"There is? Who?"

"Mr. N."

Josh thought he must have heard wrong. "Mr. N? Um, I don't think so. He's so antitech, I don't think he even owns a cell phone."

Ms. Hernandez laughed. "I wouldn't be so sure if I were you. Remember that instructor I told you about? The one who introduced me to 'The Zen of Python'?"

"The computer whiz and one-of-a-kind . . . Wait a minute." Josh's jaw dropped. "You were talking about *Mr. N*?"

She nodded, then leaned in and whispered, "He doesn't like anyone to know, but he's a genius with computers. My last year in college, I was struggling to master Python and Java. He tutored me for three months and I aced the classes. He helped me get my first job in the tech field, too."

Josh knew Ms. Hernandez volunteered at the school because it was important to help kids learn the right way to use computers—something else Mr. N had taught her, apparently.

"I don't understand," Josh said. "Why would he keep all that a secret? If I was a computer genius, I'd shout it from the rooftops!"

"I'm sure you would, just as I'm sure he has his reasons for *not* shouting it. You'd have to ask him what those reasons are, though."

Their conversation was cut short when other students arrived. Josh loved the club, but today his mind was buzzing too much to concentrate.

Mr. N is a computer whiz? No way.

When he heard the second bell ring, he raised his hand. "Ms. Hernandez? Would it be okay if I skipped the group today?"

She laughed. "Go ahead, Josh. And good luck."

He grabbed his laptop and backpack, dashed through the library and across the hallway, and zipped out the front doors just in time to climb aboard bus number three.

He found a seat, and after catching his breath, he texted Vanessa.

> Got a surprise for you . . .

> Call me NOW!!

> I'm on the bus. Will call from home.

> WHAT?? CodeBoy Skips Python Club??? Is the world ending?

> Lol. Talk soon

The bus ride seemed to take hours, and when Josh got home he walked straight to the kitchen table.

His dad called from upstairs, "Hi, Josh."

"Hi, Dad."

"Mom and Sophie are with Gramma this afternoon, and I'm catching up on emails. I don't know if there are snacks or anything."

"No problem—I'll find something." He helped himself to a bag of chips. He'd just started munching when his phone buzzed. He checked the screen, then shook his head. Vanessa was terrible at waiting. For anything.

He stuffed another chip in his mouth and answered the phone: "I said I'd call you."

She said, "Are you talking with your mouth full?"

He swallowed. "No."

"Liar. I knew you'd get a snack before calling me. That's why I called you."

Josh laughed. "Okay, okay. . . . Are you sitting down?"

He heard rustling. "I am now."

"Good. So here's the surprise. Ms. Hernandez, my coding teacher, said she had a fantastic tutor when she was in college, a grad school genius who might help us track down the pirate, *and* it's someone who works at our school—guess who!"

"Um . . . Mrs. Fusaro?"

"Nope."

"Mrs. Coleman?"

"No," Josh said, "it's *Mr. N!*"

"Get *out!*" Vanessa cried. "She's messing with you."

"No," he said. "Ms. Hernandez isn't like that. But you get what this means, right?"

"Yeah. Person X and Person Z have another secret about Person Y."

That brought Josh up short. "Oh. I guess that's true. But I meant we have a new lead about Mr. N before he came to Clara Vista. If we can figure out where Ms. Hernandez went to college, and when she graduated, then *that* will give us a definite place and time to add to the Frindle Files."

Silence.

"To add to *what?*" Vanessa said.

"To the Frindle Files. I keep everything I find out about Mr. N in a folder on my laptop called the Frindle Files."

"Oh. Right. Of course you do."

Josh went on. "Well, I did. I moved it into the trash last night. But I'm going to move it back to my desktop. And before you say anything, I know we agreed not to dig into his past any more. But that was before we had the awesome clue to follow."

"And we will follow it, eventually. But first, I have an important question: How are X and Z going to get Y's help tracking down the pirate without revealing that they know Y's a computer genius?"

It was a good question, and Josh didn't have the answer. Not yet.

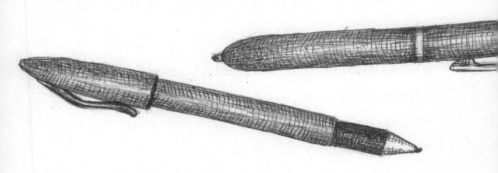

Chapter 21

For Wilbur

The idea came to Josh that night as he completed his list of *The Elements of Style* e-book errors. Neatly. In blue ink. He slipped the paper into his backpack and clicked out of the pirated book.

"The worst bunch of bits and bytes ever," he muttered, remembering how Mr. N had described the e-book that day. Then he remembered something Ms. Hernandez had said, about how the pirate didn't bother to correct the mistakes.

Does that mean there's a way to correct them? If so, wouldn't an ELA teacher—and secret computer genius—who loves The Elements of Style *want to fix them?*

"It could work," Vanessa said when he explained his idea on the way to room 113 Tuesday morning. "Then again . . .

it could be a total wipeout. I'm talking skimboard face-plant times ten!"

"I'm willing to take that risk." He smiled and raised both fists overhead. "For Wilbur!"

"For who? Oh, you mean the pig in *Charlotte's Web*." She grinned back. "But if we're going to have a rallying cry for this mission, shouldn't it be *For Grammar*?"

He made a horrified face. "You're kidding, right?"

"Duh." She laughed and lifted her fists over her head too. *"For Wilbur!"*

Josh's plan was simple—not complex, not complicated, and he hoped it wouldn't end in chaos. It depended on Mr. N collecting their homework at the start of class. Vanessa volunteered to make that happen.

"Mr. N?" She raised her hand. "Can we turn in our e-book error lists now? Mine took me so long to do, I don't want anything to happen to it."

"Good idea," he said. "Everyone, please pass your papers to the front of your rows."

As his classmates dug around in their backpacks, Josh raised his hand.

"Yes, Josh?"

Josh stood up. "I just wanted to apologize to everyone for that e-book. Especially to you, Mr. N."

"Thank you, Josh," Mr. N said.

But Josh wasn't done. "It's too bad there isn't a way to use the lists we made."

Mr. N frowned. "What do you mean?"

"We've done all the work finding the mistakes. I wish we could correct them in the e-book. But we can't . . . can we?"

"We could, actually," Mr. N said thoughtfully. "But it involves some sophisticated computer skills. And I'm afraid I don't have time to teach those skills in this class."

"Oh." Josh pretended to be disappointed. On the inside, he was dancing a jig. Mr. N had just let it slip that he knew how to fix the mistakes—and how to teach sophisticated computer skills!

So he was excited. And he was relieved, too. If Mr. N had decided to make the class correct the errors, Josh would never hear the end of it!

Now he sank back into his seat. "So I guess there's nothing at all we can do about that stupid e-book. It'll be out there. Forever. With E. B. White's name on it." He looked around at his classmates. "You guys know E. B. White also wrote *Charlotte's Web,* don't you?"

Liam spoke up from the second row. "I do, but only because you mentioned it in your interview on Miguel's YouTube channel."

"I remember that book," said Brendan. "It made me cry! It's about a pig named Wilbur, right?"

"And a spider named Charlotte," Charlotte added, grinning.

Rachel snorted. "I read it when I was seven. It's a book for babies."

"Then I guess I'm a baby," Miguel said. "Because I read it this weekend, and I thought it was awesome!"

As more students chimed in with their opinions on *Charlotte's Web*, Mr. N put down the stack of homework papers and opened a desk drawer. For a second, Josh thought he was getting out his red pen to put marks by their names for speaking out of turn.

To his shock, Mr. N withdrew a laptop and opened it on his desk. Then he moved toward the chalkboard. But instead of picking up a piece of chalk, he pushed the board aside—and started rolling up the parts-of-speech posters that covered the whiteboard!

The class fell silent. Students glanced at one another in confusion. *What's going on?* those looks asked.

Josh and Vanessa exchanged looks too. But theirs were hopeful.

Mr. N returned to his desk and held up their homework assignments.

"We can't correct these errors. But there might be a way we can remove the e-book itself from the internet." He looked around the room. "What do you say? Who wants to give it a try?"

Every hand flew into the air.

"For Wilbur!" Josh shouted.

"For Wilbur!" the others echoed.

Mr. N shushed them. But he was smiling. "It seems we have a slogan," he said. He pulled a remote from his desk drawer and pushed a button. The whiteboard lit up. "Now let's get to work."

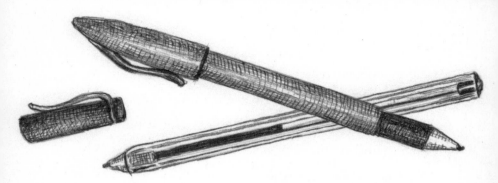

Chapter 22

To Catch a Pirate

Mr. N fired up his laptop. It connected with the whiteboard. Now whatever he did on his computer showed up on the big screen.

"So far this year," Mr. N said, "we've focused our writing on descriptions. Plus one paragraph about keeping a secret." He grinned. "That was a frindy assignment, wasn't it?"

The class groaned.

"Now we're going to do something different: a persuasive piece. A letter, to be more specific. Something that will convince whoever put that e-book on the internet to take it down. And instead of each of you writing your own, we're going to write our persuasive letter together in class. We'll spend fifteen minutes each day on it until it's ready. Then we'll email it to the person responsible for the e-book."

Josh's hand shot into the air.

"Yes, Josh?"

"How can we send an email if we don't know who the person is or what his—"

"Or her!" Vanessa interrupted.

"Or her email address is?" Josh finished.

Mr. N. nodded. "You're right. We don't have the email address. But I have an idea how to get it."

He sat at his desk and pulled his laptop closer. His fingers flew over the keyboard, opening his browser, typing in a website, and connecting to that website. He paused then and pulled up the e-book link, but he didn't open it.

"To find our email, we first need to search domain name registration records. Yes, Rachel?"

"What's a domain—whatever it was you called it?"

"A domain name is a unique internet address, like our school website's address. Registries keep records of the names—like the records towns keep of the names of licensed dogs. Make sense?"

Rachel nodded. So did a lot of other kids.

"Now, to search these records, you need the domain name." He glanced up. "Josh, perhaps you could go to the whiteboard and point to the e-book's domain name?"

Josh walked to the whiteboard and used his finger to circle the e-book's link—the one ending in .com.

"Thank you."

Vanessa flashed him a thumbs-up as he sat down. Mr. N used his cursor to highlight the domain name. Then he cut and pasted it into the search box on the website, and hit search. He did everything quickly and effortlessly, like he'd done it a million times before. Which, Josh guessed, he had.

A new page popped up on the website on the whiteboard. Josh almost leaped to his feet again. "There!" he cried. "That line that says 'Registrant Email'! Is that the person behind the e-book?"

"It could be," Mr. N said. "At the very least, that email is connected to the person in some way."

"So that's who we send the email to?" Vanessa asked.

"That's who we send the email to," Mr. N replied. He saved the search results with the click of a button, closed the site and the e-book, and shut down his laptop.

"Awwww," the class murmured.

Mr. N gave them the evil eyebrows, but below them,

his eyes twinkled. "Get out a pen and paper, please. Blue or black ink."

When everyone had their pens and paper, he pointed at Josh. "You started us on this project. So what should we do first?"

All eyes turned to him. Josh gulped. "Well, um, I guess first of all, we need a great message."

Vanessa jumped right in. "Yeah! The message has to be powerful enough to convince a pirate."

"A pirate?" Mr. N looked amused.

Vanessa smiled. "Oh, yeah. Josh figured out that the book had so many mistakes because it was pirated."

Mr. N raised an eyebrow. "Good for you for figuring that out."

Josh turned red but didn't look away. He wanted to see Mr. N's reaction to what he said next. "Actually, my coding instructor, Ms. Hernandez, told me. Do you know her?"

He thought Mr. N's eyes widened slightly. "I've seen her here after school a few times," his teacher replied.

"She's really good at coding," Josh said. "Anyway, about the message. Maybe we could start by putting our slogan in the subject line?"

Mr. N stood up and pulled the chalkboard back to the front of the class.

For Wilbur! he wrote. "Okay. What next?"

Brendan raised his hand. "My parents say it's a good idea to greet the person you're writing to, even in an email. You know, like *Dear Grandma* or *Hi, Aunt Leslie.*"

"It should be something that gets the pirate's attention," Miguel said. "How about *Hey, You Stupid Pirate!*"

Everyone laughed. Mr. N wrote *Greeting* under the slogan. "We can come up with the right words later. Yes, Charlotte?"

"I agree with Miguel—well, not about the *stupid* part. But we have to get the pirate's attention, and not just in the greeting. In the whole email."

Mr. N wrote down: *Get Attention—How?*

Josh remembered when he'd picked up *Charlotte's Web.* Just one look at the cover brought back the memory of his parents reading to him.

"Pictures!" he blurted. "Of the covers of *The Elements of Style* and *Charlotte's Web.* Because both books are important, and both were written by E. B. White. And we could include images from the e-book that show lots of errors, too."

"That'll be every page," Hunter grumbled.

Mr. N wrote *Images* under *Greeting.* "Let's add one last thing. Then we'll pick it up again tomorrow. Suggestions?"

Vanessa sprang to her feet. "I have one! Instead of sending this pirate just one email, how about we send him—"

"Or her!" Josh said.

"Or *her* a whole flood of emails? Really put the pressure on full blast!"

"We could make videos, too, about how much we want that e-book gone!" Miguel put in.

"We could get the entire sixth grade involved," Hunter said. "Maybe even the whole school!"

Josh got caught up in the excitement. "Why stop there? Let's talk to librarians and teachers and anyone who loves books and writing and . . . and . . . well, you get the idea!"

Mr. N looked amused again. "For now, we'll focus on this one email. But who knows? Everyone start drafting tonight and we'll discuss tomorrow." He glanced at the chalkboard. "For Wilbur?"

"For Wilbur!"

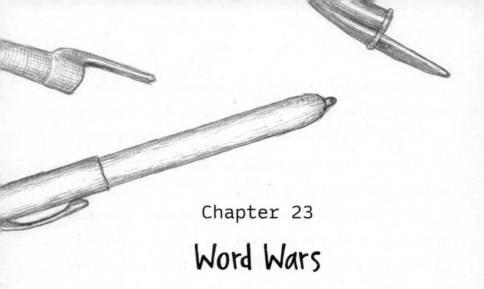

Chapter 23

Word Wars

Josh was still smiling when he took a seat next to Vanessa at lunch. He felt victorious: Mr. N and his ELA class were one hundred percent behind taking down the *Elements of Style* e-book.

He listened to Vanessa, Miguel, and Hunter bounce ideas for the email off one another. But their conversation only had about half his attention. The other half of his mind was sifting through what he'd learned about Mr. N. He felt like the different bits of information were beginning to come together—sort of like a giant jigsaw puzzle.

The frame of the puzzle had been easy. There along the right edge was Nick Allen in New Hampshire, holding up his frindle; and over near the left edge was Mr. N in

California, holding up *The Elements of Style*. But all he had out there in the middle was the clue from Ms. Hernandez, and then today's proof that Mr. N truly was a secret computer expert. Even though Josh could imagine a few fuzzy patterns, the big picture wasn't clear.

Still, he wasn't discouraged. His first Python coding instructor had made him memorize a saying: "If you take the time it takes, it takes less time." And Josh had learned how a group of program functions would suddenly click into place and make perfect sense—*if* he had given the problem enough thought and effort.

And *this* problem of the missing eight years? It was going to take more time . . . but maybe not that much.

"Hello? Earth to Josh? Do you read me?"

Josh blinked to find his friends laughing at him. "What? Oh, sorry. I was just thinking about something."

"No kidding," Vanessa said. "While you were thinking, we've been working on a great message for the email."

"I thought we were doing that in Mr. N's class."

Miguel shrugged. "Why wait? The sooner we get the message done, the sooner we can get the email sent."

"And the sooner we start putting the pressure on the pirate," Vanessa said.

"Okay," Josh said. "So what's the message?"

A bell rang, signaling the end of lunch. "No time to explain now," Vanessa told him as she gathered her things. "I'll come to your house after school. We can work on it more then. Cool?"

Josh smiled. "Cool."

🮲🮳🮲🮳 🮲🮳🮲🮳

Josh saved Vanessa a seat on bus three. She arrived like a gust of wind, blasting two hundred words a minute.

"Okay, so I've been thinking more about our *For Wilbur!* campaign. We need to come up with a new list of people to send our message to. Not just the pirate, though obviously that person is number one on the list. We get them to reach out to every single contact they can think of! And like I said, we can research other places—like libraries and newspapers and online forums and blogs and stuff."

"Whoa, whoa, whoa!" Josh held up his hands as if surrendering. He liked Vanessa's enthusiasm. But the programmer in him worried she was jumping over *simple* and going straight to *complicated.* And that wasn't a good idea.

"That all sounds great, but the most important thing

right now is the message. Because if *that* part's not right, this project won't work."

"Oh—right. Sorry. And I'm glad you're thinking about *that* part. I'll be quiet now."

"I don't want you to be quiet," Josh said. "I just want you to stop talking."

Vanessa laughed. "Right. Got it."

■□■■ ■□■□

Vanessa stared at Josh across his kitchen table. "How can you be so *dense*? Our message has to get people's attention, remember? So we need to explain all the different ways the e-book is messed up. We have to get them as upset as we are so they'll care enough to email the pirate—and not just once but over and over! Otherwise, that e-book will stay on the internet like a pile of dirty laundry." She stuck out her bottom lip. "Is that what you want, Joshua?"

They had been fighting about the email message for half an hour—arguing about what kind of words to use, and especially how many words. Josh had written a mostly friendly message, simple and short; Vanessa had written a tough message, almost angry, with loads of details.

And now Josh wanted to cover his face with both hands and scream. He was tempted to shout, *MY WAY is* RIGHT, *and YOUR WAY is* WRONG—but instantly, he knew that a binary approach to this problem was not going to help.

The truth was, there were a million different ways to say *anything*—even if you obeyed all the rules in *The Elements of Style* . . . and that gave Josh a fresh idea.

He grabbed the paperback from his backpack and said, "How about this: If we can find something in *this book* that says we should do the email *your* way, then that's what we'll do. And if we can find something that points at *my* way, then we'll go with that. Sound fair?"

Vanessa narrowed her eyes. "Why do I feel like this is a trick?"

Without smiling, Josh said, "It's not a trick. We both know that this book explains tons about good writing, and we've got a writing problem, so there ought to be stuff in here that'll help us solve it, right?"

"Yeah . . . I guess so. Can I use the laptop version, so I can search for things?"

"Sure," said Josh, "but be careful—it has a couple of mistakes."

She stuck out her tongue. "Ha ha, *so* funny. For your

information, I downloaded the e-book from the library last night."

He laughed. "Yeah, me too. Still got the nasty one, though."

"Yeah," she said. "Me too."

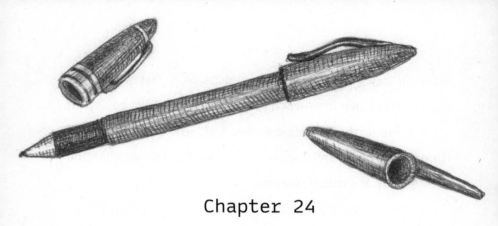

Chapter 24

On Message

It got quiet in the kitchen at the Willett house, so quiet that after ten minutes, Josh's mom called from the family room, "Is everything okay in there?"

"It's fine, Mom—we're doing some research."

Actually, Josh was done, just waiting for Vanessa to finish her searches. He could tell by the look on her face that she wasn't finding much support for the email she wanted to send.

A few minutes later, she looked up at him. "Okay, smarty-pants, tell me what you've got. Because there's *nothing* in this book about bulking up on nitty-gritty details, and there are no examples showing how to make writing sound like loud yelling. Which is still pretty much what I want to do. So, what did you find?"

Josh said, "Just a couple things, really. First, that part about 'Omit needless words.' We should be able to say all we need to with just a few sentences. Which should make it easier for people to understand. And did you see that one about 'Do not explain too much'?"

"Yeah, I saw it," she said, rolling her eyes. "And I remember it from the homework assignment. I also saw, 'Be clear.' So, *fine*—I'm wrong, and you're right. So, congratulations—you *win*."

"Don't put it like that," he said. "We want this to be good, right? So, if I say your way needs fixing, I'm only trying to make it better. Like, if you had something hanging out of your nose, and I saw it just when we were walking into the cafeteria one day, you'd want me to tell you, wouldn't you?"

That got a tiny smile.

She said, "So . . . now you're comparing the quality of my writing to a *booger*? That's very flattering, but I've had enough convincing now. Let's get this done, okay?"

It felt like they were on the same team again, and thirty minutes later their message had been written, debated some more, edited, and proofread. Two messages, actually.

The first was to whoever pirated the book:

Subject: For Wilbur!

Dear Book Pirate,

E. B. White wrote *Charlotte's Web,* and it's one of the best books *ever.*

E. B. White also worked on *The Elements of Style,* a great book about great writing.

But look at this page from your e-book of *The Elements of Style:*

> paragraph iss a con venien
> it servves all form s of lit
> As long as itt holds

See the misspellings and the other goofs? Almost the whole e-book is this bad!

For the sake of good writing and E. B. White's good name, we ask you to please do the right thing.

REMOVE THIS E-BOOK FROM THE INTERNET!

The second message was to their classmates and anyone else Mr. N agreed should get the email:

Subject: For Wilbur!

Dear People:

We are Team *For Wilbur!*—a group of sixth graders from Clara Vista, California. We've been studying *The Elements of Style,* a terrific book about great writing. One of the authors is E. B. White, who also wrote *Charlotte's Web.* Remember that book? We do, and we love it!

So when we discovered a pirated e-book version of *The Elements of Style* that's full of mistakes, we had to do something—for E. B. White, and for Wilbur!

We think it's wrong to let this e-book stay on the internet.

If you agree, we ask that you forward the attached message to everyone you know who loves *Charlotte's Web* and great writing!

Thank you, and remember, we do this FOR WILBUR!

Vanessa's dad arrived right at five o'clock to get her. As Josh walked out to the driveway with her, she said, "Do you think this is really going to work?"

He shrugged. "Hope so. I guess we'll see what everyone thinks tomorrow. It kind of depends on how much anyone really cares about *Charlotte's Web*. And E. B. White. And also about good writing. I think *I'm* starting to care more about that—good writing, I mean."

"Yeah, me too," she said. It looked like there was more she wanted to say, but her dad was rolling down the window. "See you tomorrow."

"See you."

Josh wished Vanessa hadn't had to leave—so they could've talked a little more, just talked about something besides writing.

"Omit needless words" was excellent advice for writing, and for coding, too. But Josh felt like talking needed a different rule—especially talking with Vanessa. Maybe "More words are usually better" or "There are no needless words"—especially ones like *Nice work* or *Thanks*. Those counted double, maybe triple.

Walking back into the house, Josh wondered if he could have said things better. Maybe kinder.

No question about it: more words would have been nice.

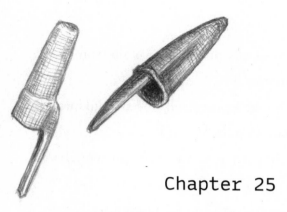

Chapter 25

Moving Forward

Mr. N's second-period class was buzzing on Wednesday morning.

Mr. N started class by announcing they'd spend the first fifteen minutes working on their *For Wilbur!* message.

Josh raised his hand.

"Yes, Josh?"

"Vanessa and I worked on the message after school yesterday. Two messages, actually. Can we share them with everyone?"

Mr. N looked surprised. Then he fired up the whiteboard and said, "I assume these messages are on your laptop?"

"Yes."

"Then connect your computer to the whiteboard so the whole class can see them."

Josh pulled out his laptop, opened both documents, and arranged them so they were side by side.

Mr. N explained how to connect to the whiteboard. "Open your laptop's general settings. Click on Wi-Fi, then touch 113wb, and your screen should automatically mirror onto the display up here, no password needed."

Seconds later, there was Josh's screen image with the two messages.

The kids started talking about them immediately. Josh tried to listen, but he was sidetracked by how smoothly Mr. N had helped him connect. One more note for the Frindle Files!

Mr. N called for attention. "Who thinks these messages sound right?"

Everyone raised their hand—including Mr. N. Vanessa turned around in her seat and pretended to high-five Josh. He grinned.

Mr. N picked up a stack of forms and passed them out. "These are permission slips saying your parents agree to let you send these emails. Have them signed tonight. Once I have them all in hand, you can move forward. Speaking of moving forward, please hold up your copies of *The Elements of Style*. Both formats!"

Usually, there were groans after this request. This time? There were cheers.

"For Wilbur!"

▋☐▋▓ ▟☐▟☐

Everyone turned in their permission slips the next morning. That night, Josh sent a text to Vanessa:

> 3 . . .

> 2 . . .

> 1!

He tapped the send button on his email. Once to shoot the message to the pirate. Then a second time to send the other message to all his contacts. He received a message himself from Vanessa:

> And done! Now what?

> Now we wait.

Josh shut down his laptop and went to bed.

Nothing more I can do!

He didn't know it, but someone else was doing something.

Miguel made a big announcement at the start of Mr. N's class the next morning.

"Yesterday afternoon, I made a video about what we're doing, and then uploaded it onto my YouTube channel. I held up my new copy of *Charlotte's Web* and talked about E. B. White, and then I—"

"Hang on, Miguel," Josh said. "Mr. N, can Miguel put his YouTube channel on the whiteboard so we can watch the video?"

Mr. N nodded and walked Miguel through the same steps Josh had gone through two days before. And just like then, Josh marveled at how easy he made it seem. A moment later, there was Miguel on the whiteboard, smiling into the camera. Behind him, one of the chairs was almost hidden by a black Labrador that looked as big as a pony.

"Hey, everybody, it's Miguel again, talking to you from beautiful Clara Vista, California. And back there? That's Watcher the Wonderdog. I'm here today to ask if you can help me and my friends fix a problem. First, *this* book is not the problem. This is *Charlotte's Web,* written by E. B. White, and it is *fantastic.* I loved it when I was eight, and I still love it now. Here's a picture of the author, E. B. White, sitting at his typewriter, and this guy was a super-genius at writing. See *this* paperback, *The Elements of Style?* This is not the problem either. This book is all about good writing, and E. B. White first heard about it when he was in college, because his professor William Strunk Jr. wrote the first edition. Then, years and years later, good ol' E.B. worked on the book, and added some new stuff of his own to it, which is why his name is on the cover. Now, here's the problem: My ELA teacher is using this paperback to teach us about writing, but sometimes an e-book can be pretty handy, right? So right here on my laptop, I've got an e-book of *The Elements of Style* that I downloaded from the internet. But take a look—this e-book is *so messed up!* All the stuff I highlighted here in blue? These are all mistakes, *hundreds* of them. They got there because this e-book was *pirated*. That's illegal, folks. And a word of warning: pirated e-books sometimes contain viruses! This one didn't, luckily. But how would you feel if someone took your work—your words—and stole them, and to make it worse—did so badly? Well, my ELA class is working on an email to send to the pirate, asking—no, *demanding*—that the e-book be deleted from the internet immediately. We hope everybody who cares about *Charlotte's Web* and good writing will join us and email the same message. *Watcher—bad dog!* Shoot, I gotta go feed Watcher before he starts eating the chair. Stay tuned for future developments—like the message we're going to send—and don't forget to give this video a thumbs-up and forward it to everybody you know! Thanks a bunch, and catch you later! *Down, Watcher!*"

Miguel paused the video just as his Labrador jumped into his lap. A burst of applause and laughter filled the classroom.

Miguel blushed and said, "Thanks. Yeah, so, the best

part is here in my YouTube channel analytics." He navigated around the screen from the keyboard, opened another screen, and then lit up a tab called Overview. "I put this video up about fifteen hours ago, and it's already been viewed more than *seven thousand* times, plus it's got almost six thousand shares! That's the most views *ever* for something on my channel, and that sharing rate? *Huge!* I'm not gonna say the V-word—okay, I am. Even if it doesn't go *viral,* this message is going to grab a *lot* of eyeballs—like, *big-time!*"

Vanessa started to ask something, but a loud *bong* from the intercom cut her off.

"Excuse me, Mr. Nicholas—this is Mr. Ortega. Can you hear me?"

"Yes, I'm here."

"Good. Sorry to interrupt your class, but I have a quick question. Did you recently use your school email address to send out some information about a pirated e-book?"

All the kids looked at the speaker below the clock—except for Josh. He watched Mr. N.

"Yes," he said. "I reached out to some colleagues yesterday. It's part of a class project, and we were just talking about it."

No sound but a hum from the speaker for a full five seconds. Josh kept his eyes on Mr. N's face.

Then Mr. Ortega coughed a little, and said, "I see. Please put that project on hold right now, and I'll be there at your room in ten minutes or less."

Anyone else watching Mr. N during those seconds of silence might not have spotted anything, but Josh wasn't anyone else. He had become an expert at reading Mr. N's face, and he had seen the tiniest hint of a smile.

The intercom clicked off, and a gush of whispers flooded the room.

Something big was about to happen—in ten minutes or less.

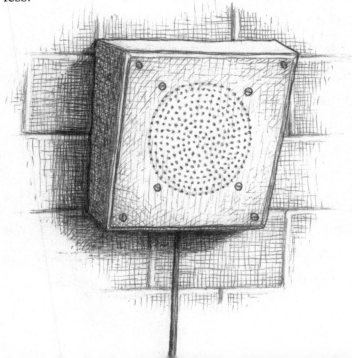

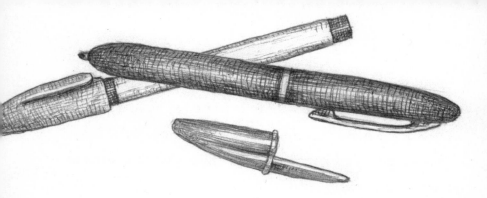

Chapter 26

Going Viral

Mr. Ortega hurried into room 113 exactly three minutes and twelve seconds later—Josh was timing it on his phone.

Mr. N stood to the left of his desk, and the principal walked up and stood to the right of it. He nodded at Mr. N and then at the class, but he didn't smile. They looked like they were about to have a duel.

"Good morning, Mr. Nicholas, and good morning, girls and boys. The first thing I should say is that normally I would speak to your teacher in private about a situation like this. But since this involves a class project, I need to talk with all of you. I am here because of two things that have come to my attention. First, our school secretary told me about a message she noticed this morning from someone that she follows online—a novelist who has more than five million followers."

He pulled a piece of paper from his pocket and began to read.

" 'A bunch of sixth graders in Clara Vista, California, need your help!' "

Mr. Ortega pointed at Mr. N and said, "And then at the bottom of the post is your school email address. There is also a link to a video." He glanced at the whiteboard, still paused on Miguel and Watcher, and scowled. "That video, to be exact."

Miguel gasped. "For real? Five million people have info about my YouTube channel?" He looked like he might faint.

The principal ignored him and turned toward Mr. N. "I had just learned about the post when I got a call from Mr. Carver at the computer operations center for Clara Vista schools, and he said that your school email account received more than twelve thousand emails between nine last night and nine this morning, and emails are still arriving at more than two hundred per hour. He told me that our servers may run out of space and that our system and all our school websites could crash at any moment."

Mr. Ortega put the paper away and looked at the entire

class. "And now I am here to tell all of you that this project is officially over."

Mr. N walked around his desk and stood beside the principal.

He said, "Thanks for sharing this, Mr. Ortega. Josh Willett and Vanessa Ames are the student leaders on this project, so they should be the first ones to respond. They have my full support."

Josh's pencil skidded across the paper where he had been taking notes. Half-panicked, he looked from Mr. N's face to the principal's.

Mr. Ortega frowned. "You must not have understood me, Mr. Nicholas. I am not inviting a discussion here. I am *ordering* everyone who is involved in this project to stop all activity right now."

That thin smile on Mr. N's face? It didn't fool Josh—or the principal. Things were about to get rough.

Josh called out, "Mr. Ortega?"

The interruption surprised everyone—including Josh himself.

The principal didn't take his eyes off Mr. N, but he angled toward Josh and said, "Yes? What is it?"

"Um . . . well, I just thought you'd like to know more

about the project before you shut it down. Maybe you could look at the e-book and see for yourself why we're upset?"

At Mr. N's nod, Miguel disconnected from the white-board and Josh clicked his way back on. He pulled up the pirated e-book and opened to a random page. On the big screen, the errors seemed to leap out at him.

Mr. Ortega scanned the page and pursed his lips. "Is this the approved e-book from the library?"

"No, sir," Josh replied. "I downloaded it from the internet."

"I did too," Vanessa piped up.

"Me too," other voices echoed.

"We all have the school copy now, though," Josh added.

Mr. Ortega didn't say anything. The room fell quiet. Then the silence was interrupted by a loud burp.

The principal glared around the room. "*Who did that?* I demand to know *right now!*"

Miguel stood up. "It was me . . . except it wasn't *actually* me, only sort of." He gestured to his laptop. It was still open to his YouTube analytics page. "I get that alert sound on my phone when something special happens with one of my YouTube videos. And the video I made about that e-book? It's really taking off!"

"Taking off?" said Mr. Ortega. "What do you mean?"

"Well, if you look at the views—wait, I'll put it on the whiteboard and open up the real-time window." Miguel took over the screen again. "Okay, see those green lines on the right? That's how many views my video got during every minute for the last hour, and it refreshes every ten seconds, so there at the far right side, that's the leading edge, and this puppy is turning into a *monster,* and it's *spiking—* like, *big-time!"*

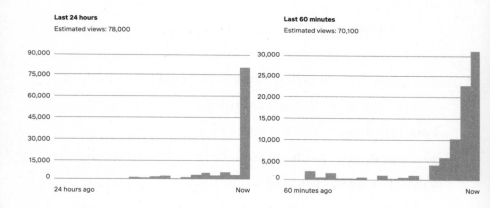

Last 24 hours
Estimated views: 78,000

Last 60 minutes
Estimated views: 70,100

Mr. Ortega looked so frustrated he was practically shouting. "Tell me what all that *means!* I don't understand a word you are saying!"

Mr. N said, "Excuse me, Mr. Ortega. Miguel's just excited. The graph shows how many times his video has been viewed since it was posted fifteen hours ago. The big news is the graph on the right. More than seventy thousand of those views have happened during the last hour. And what all of it means is simple: This project you're telling us to stop? It's not ours anymore. These kids—with their parents' permission—told the truth about something that needs to change . . . and the words are out there now. They can't be stopped. We can watch what happens, but we can't slow it down or make it go backward. And if *I* were the principal of this school, I'd put out a press release about our brilliant students and how carefully and bravely they're using their voices to protect the world from bad grammar, to speak up about the importance of language . . . and to root out pirated e-books!"

Looking at Mr. Ortega's face, Josh thought he might keep on yelling.

Instead, the principal took a deep breath. "Let me see that e-book again. And I'll need a copy of the paperback."

Vanessa raised her hand. "You can borrow mine, sir!"

She jumped up and handed him her *Elements of Style* and her laptop with the e-book on the screen.

The classroom went completely still while Mr. Ortega swiped through the e-book and flipped through the paper-back. After a few minutes, he returned both to Vanessa and asked to see the emails. Mr. N showed them to him on his computer.

The principal read quickly. He looked up at Mr. N. Then he turned and faced the class.

"I owe you an apology. When I came rushing in here, it's clear that I didn't know the actual situation. Thank you for explaining what you're doing, and I want you to keep up the good work. Now, if you'll excuse me, I have to go write a press release—and if I need help with it, I know where to come!"

Vanessa jumped up and began to clap, and in two seconds the whole class was up—a full standing ovation.

Mr. Ortega smiled, turned and shook hands with Mr. N, and then left the room. And after the door closed behind him, Miguel's phone made another loud burp.

His video had just hit 85,000 views.

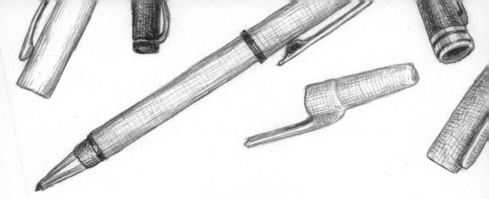

Chapter 27

Journalism

"Wait—I have to get off!"

The bus driver looked at Josh in his mirror and shook his head. "Sit down, *now.*"

Josh hurried back to his seat, got out his phone, and took a photo of a blue van in the school parking lot with a huge logo on its side: KCBS 2 NEWS.

Changing his aim, Josh snapped three people walking toward the front doors—a woman wearing a gray suit, a younger woman carrying a camera and a tripod, and a tall guy wearing a Dodgers cap and holding a backpack in one hand and a large microphone in the other.

Josh sent a text to Vanessa.

> You still at school??

> On the bus. Why?

> TV crew from CBS 2 just arrived. Saw them as we pulled out of the parking lot.

> Cool. So we should actually watch TV news tonight!

"Josh? It's starting."

Josh hurried into the family room and sat beside his mom on the couch.

"Does this have anything to do with the permission slip I signed the other night?" she asked.

"It might," he said mysteriously. "But that's all I'm going to tell you. Don't want to ruin the surprise—and you always say how it's good to be patient, right?"

"My life was a lot easier when you were Sophie's age."

After stories about an emergency airplane landing, a fiery truck crash, four different crimes, three traffic jams, and six celebrity sightings—plus twelve muted commercials and three texts from Vanessa—Josh had become the impatient one.

He muted the TV again and said, "Is the news always like this?"

"Always," his mom said with a sigh. "Whatever we're waiting for could show up anytime between now and six-thirty, or maybe tomorrow morning, or maybe never. Just because they *have* a story doesn't mean they broadcast it."

"That stinks," he said.

Josh unmuted as the woman at the anchor desk said, "Right after this break, Bonnie Carling pays a visit to Clara Vista Middle School. Stay with *CBS 2 News at Five.*"

His mom said, "Our patience is about to pay off!"

"Yeah, this is it!" And then he muted again.

Josh's phone buzzed with a text from Vanessa, checking to be sure he was watching, then again with a message from Miguel—his video had topped 170,000 views and was still climbing.

The kitchen door slammed, and Sophie trotted in. Josh's dad followed with pizza and plates. "Anybody hungry?"

Sophie went straight for the remote.

"Play *Bluey*, play *Bluey*!"

Josh held the remote out of reach. "No, Sophie, we have

to watch something else first, and then *Bluey*—but only if you're quiet."

Josh's dad handed Sophie a picture book and a bag of jumbo Legos—which was good timing because the commercials had ended and the news anchors were back.

Josh unmuted and took a big bite of pizza just as the next segment began:

"I'm Bonnie Carling, reporting from Clara Vista Middle School in southern LA County. This is Mr. Ramon Ortega, who has been the principal here for the past twenty-four years. Mr. Ortega, I understand that some of your students have launched an email and YouTube campaign to take down a . . . pirate? Do I have that right?"

Mr. Ortega smiled at her. "Not exactly, at least not the kind you might be thinking of. A book pirate, Bonnie. Someone who puts e-books online without permission. That's illegal, of course."

Now he beamed at the camera. "Our students discovered an error-filled downloadable version of *The Elements of Style*—a famous book about writing by William Strunk Jr. and E. B. White. They were rightfully upset. So, under the guidance of their ELA teacher and with their parents' permission, they set out to demand the e-book be removed. Permanently."

He turned solemn. "So if you receive an email with the subject line *For Wilbur!*, I hope you will pay attention to it . . . and help these students with their cause."

The location shifted, and now the reporter stood by herself with *The Elements of Style* in one hand and *Charlotte's Web* in the other.

Josh pointed. "See that, where she's standing? That's the hallway outside Mr. N's room!"

Sophie whispered, *"Quiet, or no* Bluey!*"*

"This is *The Elements of Style,* and it is the classic textbook Principal Ortega just mentioned. E. B. White, the famous author of *Charlotte's Web,* knew of this writing book when he took a college class from its author, William Strunk. Many years later, E. B. White revised the book, and many people now call it *Strunk and White.* Through the years, it has sold more than ten million copies.

"I'm walking into a sixth-grade classroom here at Clara Vista Middle School, and this is Mr. Allen Nicholas. Mr. Nicholas, when you and your ELA students began this campaign to get an e-book removed, did you have any idea that the project would cause such a stir?"

"That was never the goal, and to be clear, this effort began with my students, two of them in particular. They decided it was just plain wrong that an e-book about grammar and good writing should be breaking so many of its own rules. And they decided to do something about it."

"Well, you and your students have the full support of this news station."

She addressed the camera. "If you want to help, please reach out to the contact information seen at the bottom of your screen. It's a hotline and email we set up just for this project," she added with a smile at Mr. N. "We heard there was a little problem with the school email system, so we decided to help out."

"Thank you. My students are going to be very excited to see this news report—and about any additional support they receive because of it."

"Before we go, may I ask you another question, Mr. Nicholas?"

"Sure."

"Did your name used to be Nicholas Allen, and did you grow up in Westfield, New Hampshire?"

Josh leaned forward as the camera zoomed in on Mr. N's face. It was plain that this question was totally unexpected, but he managed an awkward smile anyway.

"I am guessing you already know the answer to your question, Ms. Carling. Yes, I was born in Westfield, New Hampshire, and back then my name was Nicholas Allen."

"I'm sorry to surprise you this way, but I had to ask. A researcher at CBS 2 discovered your name change, and this young woman told me that your original name is associated with a word she had never seen before—"

"Yes," said Mr. N, nodding slowly. *"Frindle."*

Sophie's head bobbed up. She pointed at the TV, screeched, *"Frizzle!"*—and then clamped both hands over her mouth as the reporter kept talking.

"But the word *frindle* was *not* new to me, Mr. Nicholas. I was in fifth grade at a school near Chicago, and when my friends and I found out that we could stop using the word *pen* and use a completely new word instead, we did it—we *all* did it. Back then, I didn't think about where *frindle* had come from, or who had invented it. And really, that was the best part. It seemed like we had discovered the word all by ourselves, and if we didn't keep on using it, it would die. And *frindle* did become a real word—*our* word. That experience had a big impact on my childhood, and it still means a lot to me today. And just here in the Los Angeles area, there could be a million other people who would want to join me and say, thank you for inventing *frindle.*"

With both those secrets suddenly made public, Josh thought Mr. N might be upset, or at least annoyed. But as the camera zoomed in on his face again, there was nothing but warmth in his smile.

"You're very welcome . . . except your *frindle* experience didn't happen only because of me. If it hadn't been for my fifth-grade teacher, you never would have heard that word. So, really, we should both be thanking *her*."

"And what is your teacher's name?"

"Mrs. Lorelei Granger."

Mrs. Lorelei Granger

Chapter 28

Conspiracy

Josh shivered. He turned up the heat on the passenger side of the car, but he knew it wasn't just the cool October morning that had him feeling chilled.

An hour earlier it had seemed like a great idea to get to school early so he could talk with Mr. N. But now Josh was wishing he had stayed home to wait for the bus—or better yet, pretended he was sick and stayed home all day.

They stopped at a red light, and his mom said, "You saw him in that interview, honey—I'm sure he's not mad at you. Taking down that e-book is a good thing, and it's not your fault that someone did a thorough job researching Mr. N's life. And based on everything else you told us last night, I think he might be glad that all this is finally out in the open."

"Yeah, maybe so."

Josh said that, but he still felt awful. Who had led the attack to get laptops into Mr. N's classroom, who had downloaded the pirated e-book, and who had started the big push to get rid of it? One kid. And if he hadn't done those things, then Mr. N never would have been interviewed. All by himself, Josh had destroyed the privacy that Mr. N had tried so hard to protect.

Seconds after Mr. N's TV interview had ended last night, Josh's phone had exploded with texts, first from Vanessa, and then from about fifty other kids. He'd had to shut it off so he could answer the blast of questions from his mom and dad.

He had explained everything, from the Frindle Files, to Mr. N's handwritten assignments, to pirated e-books. Josh also told how he and Vanessa had chosen to keep Mr. N's secrets to themselves—which was why the end of his interview had been a huge surprise.

His mom turned into the school driveway and pulled up near the main entrance.

"I've been meaning to ask—do you still have the frindle you borrowed from me?"

"No, I put it back."

"Good—it was special to me before all this. Now it's even more so. Now, stop worrying, and have a happy day, okay? I love you, Josh."

"Love you too, Mom, and thanks for the ride."

It was ten minutes before the bus arrivals when Josh walked into the school, so he had to check in at the office. Walking out into the hallway, he thought, *I really should have stayed home.* And since he'd been awake the night before until almost midnight, faking a little sickness would have been a snap.

He turned the corner into the sixth-grade hallway and almost tripped over Vanessa, sitting on the floor with her back against the lockers.

She looked at him. "Well, look who finally showed up!"

"What are you doing here?"

"I had a hunch you'd come early. . . . Plus my dad got a text. From your mom."

"Oh—nice. A conspiracy of worriers."

She smiled and said, "I prefer to call it supportive sharing."

Josh scowled, but he was actually glad to see her. Talking to Mr. N was going to feel a lot easier with both of them there.

She got up and said, "So, next stop room one-thirteen, right?"

"Right."

They walked down the long hall and passed Mrs. Fusaro's room, neither of them talking.

Then they turned the last corner, and Vanessa said, "This is as far as I go."

"*What?* No, you should come too!"

"Nope. The Frindle Files are on *your* laptop, not mine. Just go talk with him."

"But what if he's had twelve hours to think about all this, and now he's ready to bite someone's head off?"

"He's not that kind of person—you know that. Just talk."

"Okay. But you'll come in soon, right?"

"Soon-*ish*. I'll be in the library."

Vanessa turned and walked back around the corner, and Josh listened as the sound of her footsteps got softer and softer. He stood still, waiting till he couldn't hear them at all.

She wasn't coming back, and they both knew it.

Josh turned, took a deep breath, and made himself walk the last thirty-seven steps to room 113—he counted them.

And then he made himself open the door.

Chapter 29

The Missing Pieces

osh knocked as he stuck his head into the classroom.

"Mr. N? Hi."

"Hey—come on in, Josh, and leave the door open. I was hoping to talk to you sometime today. I'm sure you and Vanessa saw the news report—you guys hit a home run! Sounds like there's a real wave of support behind *For Wilbur!*"

Josh said, "Well, Miguel had a lot to do with it, and the emails you sent helped too. But thanks." He reached Mr. N's desk. "The pirated e-book is still online, though."

Mr. N nodded. "Well, progress doesn't always happen quickly. Give it time."

Josh didn't know how to start in about the *frindle* stuff.

He felt like he was breathing too fast, and he wanted to say, *Well, thanks again—see you later!* and then blast out of there.

But he took a deep breath and steeled himself. If he could just get started, maybe he could find a way to apologize for causing Mr. N so much trouble.

"Um . . . Vanessa has been dying to know why you changed your name."

Mr. N started laughing. "As much as you were dying to know about my Hawaiian shirts?"

Josh ducked his head, feeling sheepish. "I did like learning about that, actually."

"Well, the name change isn't that complicated— I wanted to stop being known as 'that kid who made up a new word.' Even at college, people who found out kept expecting me do something else. So after freshman year at UMass, I flipped my name around and transferred to a school three thousand miles away, which helped a lot. I've also kept off the internet as much as possible—zero social media. Staying unconnected from the *frindle* phenomenon took some work, but it was worth it to me."

Josh wasn't exactly sure *why* Mr. N wouldn't want people to know who he was, but he could tell he was being honest. "After that reporter told everything about *frindle* and your name change, I thought you'd be mad, but you didn't even look annoyed—how come?"

Mr. N shrugged. "I guess I've known from the start that those facts couldn't stay hidden forever. I had tried to keep out of sight, but even so, the internet never forgets *anything*. It was always just a matter of time.

"Besides," he continued, "I'm proud of *frindle*. I had forgotten that I used to feel that way."

Josh nodded slowly, trying to fit all the pieces together. "Ms. Hernandez mentioned that you had been her programming tutor. Is that what you were doing all those years since college?"

"No, that came much later. After I graduated, I got a job working for a big software company. I can't tell you which one because my projects were top secret."

He was quiet for a moment, lost in the memory. Josh was quiet too.

That's why I couldn't find anything about him on the internet. He stayed off on his own—and the software company didn't let him talk about his work!

Then Josh said, "But if you had a top-secret software job, how come you're *here* teaching language arts?"

Mr. N reached for the dictionary on his desk and opened

the front cover. Josh saw three or four pieces of paper, and Mr. N took one out, unfolded it, and handed it to him.

"That's from the teacher I mentioned on TV last night—go ahead and read it."

"Out loud?"

"Sure."

The letter was written in flowing cursive—neatly, in blue ink—and Josh began to read.

January 18, 2013
Westfield, New Hampshire

Dear Nicholas—

Your letter was a happy surprise. I have seen your father at the hardware store now and then, and he had kept me informed about your successful work in the technology industry.

I was sorry to learn that working in that field was less enjoyable than you had hoped. Perhaps your new position as a programming tutor will prove to be a better fit. I must say that I was not surprised when you described how some of your students struggle with basic writing skills. You might offer a lecture called "Grammar and Composition for Computer

Wizards." I'm joking, of course, but truly, knowing how to craft a sentence well would make a person better at writing anything—including computer programs.

I would not say this to many of my former students, but I believe you could become an excellent middle school English teacher. You have patience, good humor, courage, and self-discipline, and younger students always offer the kind of challenges that keep one's life fresh and progressive. Teaching is a wonderful way of life, a humble life of service. One never has a doubt whether one's time is being well spent. Being able to help another person, especially a young person, to take forward steps in life? One cannot ask for a higher purpose than that. It can be exhausting, but it is remarkably satisfying. It certainly was for me.

Your father also told me that you and Janet Fisk were married last June, and I send each of you my warmest congratulations! And the next time you come to Westfield for a visit, you must stop by my house for an after-school snack. Ha, ha!

I know you will do well in any new adventure, and I hope to hear from you again when you have a free moment—which I suspect will be almost never.

With fond best wishes,
Mrs. Granger

Josh looked up at Mr. N. "Wow—so you took her advice!"

"Well, not immediately. But I did some volunteer tutoring at a local middle school, and I liked it. And . . . here I am."

"But if you were so into tech and programming and stuff, I don't get why you never wanted laptops in your classes."

For a brief instant, the evil eye appeared, and Josh thought he was about to get kicked out of the room. Then it vanished, and Mr. N sighed.

"If I could, I would take away every screen from you and all your friends for at least another three years. I'm trying to teach good writing here, and good writing demands clear thinking, and clear thinking can't happen when kids are distracted. I know for a fact that screens are a distraction, even addictive, because I've met a lot of the people who make those devices, and they make them that way on purpose—it's how they keep making billions of dollars."

He shook his head. "Those same people try to keep *their* kids away from screens for as long as possible. So that should tell you something!" He took a breath and gave Josh half a smile. "Sorry—that's the *second* time I've snapped at you about laptops. It's just . . . it's complicated."

Josh's phone vibrated in his jacket pocket—and they both heard it. He gulped and said, "Can I look at that? I think it's Vanessa. In the library."

"Sure, go ahead."

Josh looked, and laughed out loud. "She wants to know if the frindle made you rich. And she also wrote, 'Ask him where he learned to dance.' . . ."

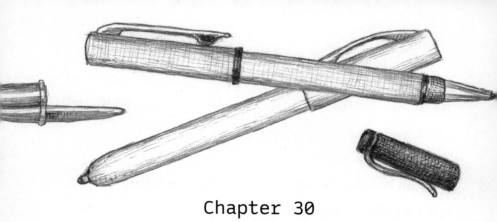

Chapter 30

All the Moves

Mr. N laughed out loud at Vanessa's text. Then he held out his hand. "Here—I'll text her back."

> Mr. N here! I have a wife I love, and a wonderful, healthy daughter. We have a safe place to live, kind relatives and friends, plus food, clothes—all the necessities. I get to work with smart kids and dedicated teachers every day. All this means I am one of the richest people in the world! So, now that you know how lucky I am, can you blame me for dancing now and then?

Vanessa texted back one word:

Genius!

Josh and Mr. N both laughed again, and there was another vibration.

Josh said, "She also wants to know—"

Mr. N said, "*Stop!* Tell her to just get down here!"

As Josh sent the text, the first bell sounded, which
meant he had about four minutes before kids would arrive
in the sixth-grade hall.

Only seconds later, Josh heard hurried footsteps—
Vanessa must have run all the way! But it was Mrs. Coleman who stepped into the room.

"Oops! Didn't know you were busy."

Mr. N said, "No, that's okay. What can I help you with?"

"Just wanted to say I *loved* your interview, and I am
thrilled to tell you that *I* was a total frindle geek—my friends
and I drove our teachers *wild*! See you later!"

And she was off down the hall again.

Mr. N smiled, then closed his eyes and pretended to
meditate, whispering, "Serenity now, serenity now, serenity
now." Then he opened his eyes and winked at Josh. "I guess

I'm going to have to get used to that sort of thing. But it'll die down soon—I hope."

Vanessa arrived, flushed and panting.

"Please sit down and catch your breath, Vanessa."

Vanessa sat, but she didn't wait. "Mr. N, what got you so hooked on *The Elements of Style*?"

"To write good code with a language like Python or Java, first you have to learn all the functions and the correct syntax and rules. You master all that, you study good and bad examples, and *then* you can start exploring your own ideas. And that's *exactly* how *The Elements of Style* is structured—I got to know the book really well thanks to two different high school teachers I had."

Josh heard a distant locker slam shut, then another one. He was running out of time. If he was going to truly apologize to Mr. N, it had to be now.

"The main reason I came in early is to say that I'm really—"

"Excuse me a second, Josh. I just remembered something."

Mr. N got up and walked to the closet at the back of his room. He grabbed a book, then came back to his desk and held it up for Josh to see.

"*Tuck Everlasting?*" Josh said. "What's that for?"

"For you. I don't think you've read it, and you should—it's a great story. Here." And he handed it to Josh. "It's a thank-you gift."

"I . . . I don't understand."

"Read the inscription."

Josh thumbed to the title page and read the handwritten note:

For Person X—
Someone who chose to do the right thing.
With many thanks,
Person Y

Josh stared at Mr. N, then handed the book to Vanessa.

"Here," said Mr. N. "You should have this, too."

He reached into a pocket of his cargo pants and then handed Josh the homemade frindle.

"Wait—you *knew* I left that pen for you . . . from the very start? *How?*"

"Where do I stand every day before class?"

"In the hall."

"All right, go stand in the hall right now, and then tell me how I knew who put that frindle on my desk."

Josh got up and walked out the classroom door.

"Um . . . you peeked around the corner and saw me?"

"Nope. I was talking with Hunter that morning."

"Did someone else see me, and tell you?"

"No, and I don't have hidden cameras, either. I'm waving my right hand now—notice anything?"

A motion caught Josh's eye, and the mystery was solved.

He walked back to his chair smiling, convinced that Mr. N was *hundreds* of times smarter than he looked.

He said, "The window on your open door works like a mirror, so you watched my reflection!"

"Bingo!"

"But how did you know that *I* was Person Z?" asked Vanessa.

Mr. N smiled at her. "I could tell. And as the days went by, I was so impressed that you two weren't spreading my secrets."

Vanessa said, "We came close a couple times—especially me. I got pretty mad after what you said to Josh about that messed-up e-book."

"Yes," said Mr. N. "I saw the look on your face." Then he said, "Now *I* have a question: Whose idea was *frindy?*"

Vanessa pointed. "That was all Josh. And you knew how to kill *frindy* because of the mistake *your* teacher made when she got mad and tried to stop *frindle,* right?"

Mr. N shook his head. "Mrs. Granger didn't tell me until years later, but that wasn't a mistake at all, and she wasn't angry. She *wanted* to keep *frindle* alive, which was why she had kept on fighting it. And actually, I wasn't trying to kill *frindy* that day. My big grammar lesson? I only did that to be funny."

"Oh," Josh said, "I didn't know that." He almost added, *Maybe funny isn't really your thing. . . .* But he decided against it.

Instead he needed to say something else before time ran out, something serious.

"I still feel like that TV interview never would have happened if *I* hadn't pushed to use laptops in class, and then I *also* pushed about the e-book—"

"No," said Mr. N. "What really happened is that you made an honest discovery, and then told *one* good friend, and then both of you kept the discovery to yourselves, even when we had some strong disagreements. I couldn't be more proud of each of you." He paused, just smiling at them. Then he glanced up at the clock, and looked at Josh. "My homeroom kids will be here in about a minute—are there any other details you need . . . for the Frindle Files?"

Josh stared again, this time with his mouth hanging open.

"You knew about *that*?"

Mr. N chuckled. "I noticed the folder when you first connected your laptop to the whiteboard. Before you clicked onto the email messages, your desktop was up just for a moment."

"I have one last question," Vanessa said. "Are you going to switch back to your real name?"

"No. My wife and daughter use Nicholas as their last name too, so a change would be complicated. Allen Nicholas or Nicholas Allen—there's not much difference. And besides, all words are made up anyway, right? So who's to say that one name is more real than another one?"

Josh laughed a little, but he still felt uneasy. "You're being super nice about everything, but I still feel terrible that you're going to get tons of attention now. Aren't you going to hate it?"

Mr. N took a moment and looked from Josh to Vanessa, then back again.

"The way my secrets came out is better than anything I could have hoped. And the truth is, I don't care what others think about me as much as I used to—and I think that means I'm finally starting to grow up. And when I *do* grow up? I want to be *just* like the two of you!"

Chapter 31

The Frindle Files: Last Entries

Josh watched Mr. N carefully over the next several weeks, and he hadn't been lying that morning they had talked before school. He didn't seem to be bothered at all by the sudden crush of attention.

Because of that first interview, Mr. N was invited to appear on a whole bunch of other shows and podcasts, like *The Tonight Show* and *Good Morning America*—and he refused all of them. But resisting didn't help much, because his rejection of the fame and publicity became a huge news story all by itself.

Mr. N did finally agree to do one media interview—on Miguel's YouTube channel. The video attracted 3.5 million views in its first week.

The attention on Mr. N and *frindle* had an unexpected side effect: bookstores across the country and online kept running out of books with E. B. White's name on them—especially that slim paperback of *The Elements of Style.*

This flood of activity kept Josh busy updating the Frindle Files. He set daily alerts to search keywords—*frindle, Nick Allen,* and *Allen Nicholas*—and always found new items. Mr. N also shared whatever he could, and there was so much current information that Josh asked Vanessa to help him decide which items to include.

They agreed that these were their favorite new entries:

• An email to Mr. N from Merriam-Webster, Inc., saying that the number of lookups for the word *frindle* in their online dictionary had recently set a new seven-day record.

• A screenshot of the *New York Times* nonfiction best-sellers, showing *The Elements of Style* paperback listed at number 3.

• An email to Mr. N from Bud Lawrence, the business manager for Frindle Products, about a dramatic increase of frindle orders and shipments for the United States,

Italy, Japan, Germany, South Korea, China, Russia, Poland, and Turkey. There were also large orders for T-shirts, caps, and mugs—featuring that image of Nick Allen holding up his frindle.

• A letter to Nicholas Allen signed by two retired high school teachers who had used *The Elements of Style* as their textbook in Nick's classes—thanking him for making them proud of their careers as English teachers.

• An email from the novelist Stephen King, congratulating Mr. N and his class on their efforts to take down the pirated e-book. Mr. King was the writer who had sent that message about their campaign to his 5.1 million online followers.

• A report that Miguel had spotted in a CNN news feed: Retailers were having trouble keeping up with extremely high demand for Hawaiian shirts.

By the middle of January, life at Clara Vista Middle School had calmed down so much that Josh decided the Frindle Files were complete—at least for the time being.

It was obvious to Josh and Vanessa and all their friends

that Mr. N was enjoying his work more than ever—he slid into those goofy dance moves way too often. He was happy that his students were consulting *The Elements of Style* with more care and attention, and even happier to see steady improvement in their writing skills.

Josh was also certain that learning to think and write more clearly was helping him to write better programs in Python—just as Mrs. Granger had predicted.

Best of all, though, was the day he tried to access the link for the pirated e-book—and got this message:

```
Error 404: File Not Found
```

Meanwhile, Mr. N amended his class requirements. Now students could show either the paperback copy of *The Elements of Style* or the school-approved e-book. For the rest of the year, only a handful of students lifted their laptops into the air.

Josh Willett was not one of them.

Assignments

Coding stuff

Paper12final_final.pdf

The Frindle Files

I collected A LOT of stuff after learning about frindle. Turn the page to see some of the evidence I found. . . .

Photos

binary.pdf

Binary code is a way to represent information using only two options, like yes/no, true/false, on/off, or 1/0. Computers send and store all information using binary, and binary is what lets you interact with a computer screen.

(Like any good code, it can be used to send secret messages in real life, too. . . .)

binary_key.pdf

■ = O □ = I

A		P	
B		Q	
C		R	
D		S	
E		T	
F		U	
G		V	
H		W	
I		X	
J		Y	
K		Z	
L		!	
M		=	
N		?	
O		@	

Homework due Wednesday

Imagine that Person X has discovered a secret about Person Y—nothing bad, but something that all of X's friends would find interesting. However, X also learns that Y would rather *not* have this secret made public.

    In one or two paragraphs totaling no more than 150 words, explain what you think Person X might do with this secret, and why. Bring your final draft to class tomorrow, written in blue or black ink on lined paper. As usual, neatness counts. And don't forget about Reminder 16 from chapter five of *The Eleme*

Mr. N

Josh Willett

1. Place yourself in the background.
2. Write in a way that comes naturally.
3. Work with a suitable design.
4. Write with nouns and verbs.
5. Revise and rewrite.
6. Do not overwrite.
7. Do not overstate.
8. Avoid the use of qualifiers.
9. Do not affect a breezy manner.
10. Use orthodox spelling.
11. Do not explain too much.
12. Do not construct awkward adverbs.

Same person????

Announcement

All students are allowed to use their school-issued laptops in class from here on out. In addition, download the free version of *The Elements of Style* from the school library. If you cannot access it from home, Mrs. Krenske will be available to help before and during school on Thursday. All students must also continue to bring the paperback copy of *The Elements of Style* to class each day. *Both the book and the e-book will be needed for work in class and for homework assignments.*

WILLIAM STRUNK JR. AND E.B. WHITE — *The* ELEMENTS *of* STYLE FOURTH EDITION

Dear Mr. Allen,

Greetings from Frindle® Productions. It has been a long time, and we are so pleased to have seen a remarkable increase in demand for items in your online FRINDLE® store this quarter. We've gone back into production on a number of items, including the mugs, caps, and T-shirts, in addition to the core pen. Demand is up in both the domestic and international markets, which you can see in the latest sales statement, attached. Please don't hesitate to reach out if there is more we can do for you. With appreciation for entrusting us with your business.

All best,

Bud Lawrence

—

BUD LAWRENCE
Frindle® Productions

Vanessa Ames

Dear Nick,

What a treat it was to see your name again after all these years! And it was even more delightful to hear that you have become a teacher, and by the sounds of it, a remarkably good one! We immediately called each other to reminisce about you. Your class, as we recall, was a particularly spirited bunch!

Adele retired five years ago, and Sue just this past summer, but we still meet for lunch once a month. We were, indeed, still using *The Elements of Style* in our classrooms every year. So it is especially gratifying to see that you have carried on that legacy. Students like you make us proud to have devoted our careers to teaching.

If you are ever back in town, please let us know—you can join us for lunch.

Warmest regards,

Sus

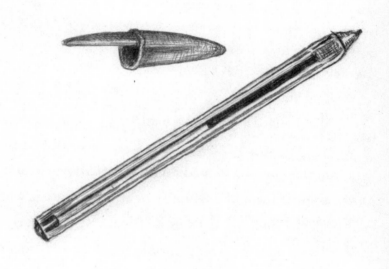

A Note from Illustrator Brian Selznick

Getting the chance to work on Andrew Clements's novel *Frindle* changed my life in so many ways. Early in my career, when I was a struggling young illustrator, I got an email out of the blue from an editor named Stephanie Lurie. She asked me if I would illustrate a new novel she was working on called *Frindle*. What was a "frindle," I wondered. The word was unusual, and probably made up, yet there was something immediately appealing and friendly in it, like I'd sort of heard it somewhere before, even though I was sure I hadn't.

I loved the story right away, and by the time I got to the end I was in tears. Looking back now, almost thirty years later, it thrills me to realize I was one of the first of the millions and millions of people who would come to have the same reaction when they read *Frindle*. With its endearing redheaded troublemaker, a deep love of language, a teacher who antagonizes her students and spends most of the time as a kind of charming villain, leading to a real celebration of the art of teaching, *Frindle* felt special to me. I immediately said yes.

The interior art was fun to draw, but the cover posed some real challenges. How would I get across the importance of . . . a pen? I eventually submitted a sketch that showed Nick standing like the Statue of Liberty, holding a ballpoint pen high over his head against a bright blue sky. I created a red frame around the whole image to make it feel more dramatic, and the work was approved by the editor and art director. But when I handed in the finished art, I got a call from the editor, telling me they were not satisfied with the image after all. It wasn't "bold" enough. They wanted something, and I quote, "more in your face!"

Confession time: I do not like redoing artwork, especially when I thought I was finished. I must admit I was a little annoyed, and I thought, "Okay, you want it 'in your face'? I'll make it 'in your face'!" And I drew Nick holding a pen and thrusting it forward, directly into "your face." And there it was, the image that's been the cover of *Frindle* for the last three decades. I knew immediately this was a *much* better cover than the one that had been rejected, and I have been deeply grateful to Stephanie Lurie ever since. I've told this story to thousands of schoolchildren over the years, and pretty much everyone agrees that it's not fun to do things over again. But look what can happen when you do! What makes me especially happy about telling this story is that it aligns with the exact sort of thing Andrew Clements himself liked to tell kids. He was an excellent rewriter and considered it a critical part of his writing process.

Initial *Frindle* cover art   The final *Frindle* cover

The impact *Frindle* has had over the years has been thrilling to see, and watching people's faces light up when they discover I did the cover is always great fun. In fact, just a few months ago I was getting coffee with a friend, and when I returned to the table with our order, my friend said, "Brian, the two young women next to us are talking about *Frindle*! They loved the book when they were young and even said how much they loved the cover." I looked over. It was clear they were still talking about the book. "What do I do?" I asked my friend. "Do I say something? Would that be strange?" Imagining how much fun it would be if an author *we* were talking about suddenly appeared, I decided to go over.

"Sorry to bother you," I said. "Were you just talking about *Frindle*?" They repeated how much they'd loved the book when they were young. "I drew that cover," I said, and after a little googling to make it clear I was telling the truth, we had the most wonderful conversation about how important the book had been to both of them. They were childhood friends who had moved to New York recently, and the serendipity of meeting me just as they were talking about their favorite childhood book was something they said they'd never forget.

Just a few weeks earlier, I'd gotten another surprising email, this time from an editor named Michelle Nagler, saying that before Andrew Clements passed away in 2019, he'd nearly completed a sequel to *Frindle*, called *The Frindle Files*. I was as floored by this news as I'm sure all of Andrew's fans were the first time they heard about the miracle of this book's existence. Looking around the coffee bar like a spy in a movie, I told the two young women that I had a secret about *Frindle* I wanted to share with them, and I let them know about the sequel. I'm so thrilled we can now share this secret with everyone.

The Frindle Files is the perfect follow-up to the first book. It feels less like a sequel and more like the logical next step. Nick has grown up, and there's a new kid, another troublemaker ready for action. But it is the ways in which the story unfolds, and the new, modern complications that ensue, that are totally surprising, and totally Andrew Clements at his very best. I only met Andrew once or twice in person, but his warmth and love were immediately apparent. Those same qualities shine through in his books, and I'm so proud to be a small part of the world of *Frindle* and his beautiful legacy. It's a legacy that I know will continue as long as there are books and stories, as well as eager students and brilliant teachers.

—Brian Selznick, February 2024

About the Author

George Clements

ANDREW CLEMENTS (1949–2019) was a *New York Times* bestselling author whose beloved modern classic *Frindle* has sold over six million copies, won nineteen state awards (and been nominated for thirty-eight!), and been translated into over a dozen languages. Before writing *Frindle*, Andrew worked as a public school teacher outside Chicago. Called the "master of school stories" by *Kirkus Reviews*, Andrew wrote over eighty acclaimed books for kids, most recently *The Friendship War* and *The Losers Club*, which *School Library Journal* called "engaging and funny . . . a laugh-out-loud first purchase" in a starred review.

andrewclements.com

About the Illustrator

BRIAN SELZNICK is the author and illustrator of many books for young people, including *The Invention of Hugo Cabret,* a winner of the Caldecott Medal and the basis for the Oscar-winning movie *Hugo,* directed by Martin Scorsese. Other titles include *Wonderstruck; The Marvels; Big Tree;* and *Baby Monkey, Private Eye,* created with Brian's husband, David Serlin. Brian has created cover art for thirteen books by Andrew Clements, plus interior illustrations for many, including *Frindle* and *The Frindle Files.* Brian and his husband divide their time between San Diego, California, and Brooklyn, New York.

thebrianselznick.com

What happens when a clever fifth grader challenges his dictionary-obsessed teacher by inventing a brand-new word, a word that—fast as lightning—spreads through the entire school, then town, then even the country? **Unexpected chaos!**

Frindle

★ "Will have readers smiling all the way through. . . . Hilarious."—*The Horn Book*, starred review

Andrew
Clements

Bestselling author with over 9 million books in print!

ILLUSTRATED BY BRIAN SELZNICK

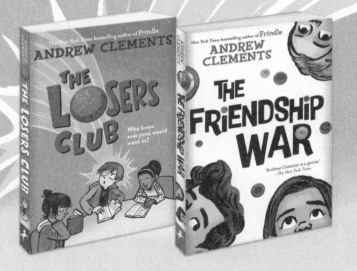